THE PASSION AND THE FLOWER

The Prince gazed down at Lokita's upturned face, then gently bent his head as his lips found hers.

It was as if he asked her to give him her heart, to allow her soul to become his.

Lokita had never experienced such feeling, such power. It was so compelling, so glorious, so brilliant—it grew in them both until it was like the blazing heat of the sun, and they stood in the center of it.

'This is love,' thought Lokita. She wanted to cry the words out loud, to dance at the glory and rapture of them.

But the Prince held her close, captive against him, kissing her with the wild intensity of a man who has come back to life from the dead . . .

Bantam Books by Barbara Cartland
Ask your bookseller for the books you have missed

Barbara Cartland's Library of Love series

Barbara Cartland's Ancient Wisdom series

Barbara Cartland

The Passion and the Flower

THE PASSION AND THE FLOWER
A Bantam Book

PRINTING HISTORY
E. P. Dutton edition published January 1978
Contempo Book Club edition published April 1978
Bantam edition / August 1978

ISBN 0-553-11690-8

Published simultaneously in the United States and Canada

*Bantam Books are published by Bantam Books, Inc. Its trade-
mark, consisting of the words "Bantam Books" and the por-
trayal of a bantam, is registered in the United States Patent
Office and in other countries. Marca Registrada. Bantam
Books, Inc., 666 Fifth Avenue, New York, New York 10019.*

PRINTED IN THE UNITED STATES OF AMERICA

Author's Note

The descriptions of Paris in 1867, the year of the International Exhibition, are all accurate, as are the references to the restaurants, the intellectuals, and the Prince Napoleon.

Lavish production was a feature of the contemporary theatre and *Cinderella* at *Théâtre Impérial du Châtelet* with its five acts and thirty scenes was as described in this novel.

Tsar Nicholas I, severe, vindictive, and mean, was undoubtedly the most alarming sovereign in Europe. In 1841 Queen Victoria wrote: "He is certainly a very *striking* man, still very handsome, his profile beautiful . . . but the expression in the *eyes* is formidable and unlike anything I ever saw before. . . . His mind is an uncivilised one."

Tsar Alexander sent a secret *Ukaze* to the Senate whereby the children of his mistress Princess Catherine Dolgoruky were given the name and rank of Prince and Princess.

Chapter One
1867

"His Highness Prince Ivan Volkonski!" a flunkey in the livery of the British Embassy announced in a loud voice.

Lord Marston, who was writing a letter, turned round from the desk at first incredulously, then sprang to his feet.

"Ivan—my dear fellow!" he exclaimed. "I had no idea you were in Paris."

"I have only just arrived," the Prince replied, "and I was delighted to be told that you were here."

"I was sent over for my sins to report to the Prime Minister on the Exhibition," Lord Marston said, "but now that you have arrived, I dare say I can neglect my duties and we can enjoy ourselves."

"We certainly will," the Prince said.

He threw himself down in one of the comfortable chairs, looking, his friend thought, more attractive and more handsome than he remembered.

Lord Marston and the Prince, who was a cousin of the Tsar, had been close friends ever since they were young men when Lord Marston's father was Ambassador to St. Petersburg.

They were of the same age, and both had been involved in various escapades in Russia, France, and

1

England which had made Society in all three countries raise their eye-brows.

But it was in fact the Prince who was the ring-leader in every outrageous adventure; for Lord Marston, conventionally English in many ways, would not on his own have embarked on such escapades.

His rather expressionless face was however smiling with pleasure and his eyes were alight as he sat opposite his friend and asked:

"Tell me, Ivan, what have you been up to now?"

The Prince's eyes were twinkling.

His eyes were in fact the most arresting part about him. They were almost purple, fringed with long, dark lashes, and revealed in their depths all the wild, passionate emotions which coursed through him.

It was perhaps chiefly his eyes which made the Prince so alluring to women that he left a trail of broken hearts behind him wherever he went.

He had almost classical features and the slim, athletic body of a man who spends a great deal of his life in the saddle.

Even among the innumerable handsome men who decorated the Tsar's Court, Prince Ivan was outstanding.

"Who is it this time who has made it necessary for you to fly from what I am sure would be a just retribution?" Lord Marston asked.

"She was in fact very delectable!" The Prince smiled. "But enough is enough, and when the Tsar was ordered by the Tsarina to remonstrate with me, I thought absence was the better part of valour."

Lord Marston laughed.

"I thought it would be a case of *cherchez la femme!* You will find plenty of your old flirts waiting for you here and a good many beauties to delight your eye."

He paused before he went on:

"As you can imagine, they have all flocked into Paris for the pickings of the Exhibition, but in consequence the place is unpleasantly overcrowded."

"That is what I expected," the Prince replied. "But I dare say, as old habitués of the most exotic haunts we will not be turned away."

"You may be quite sure of that," Lord Marston agreed dryly.

The Prince was not only enormously rich, he was exceedingly generous.

Whoever else would not be able to obtain a box at the Theatre, the best table in a restaurant, a welcome in every aristocratic mansion, it would not be Prince Ivan.

"How is Russia?" Lord Marston enquired.

"Uncomfortable!" the Prince answered briefly.

Lord Marston looked surprised.

"What has happened now? I thought everything would be roses in the garden after the Emancipation Manifesto had been signed, giving the serfs their freedom."

The Prince's expression was suddenly serious.

"The Golden Age was regarded as a permanency," he replied, "but the peasants do not understand the responsibility of ownership."

"I was present, if you remember, on the Sunday when the proclamation was read in the Churches, and Alexander was hailed as the Tsar-Liberator," Lord Marston said. "I can still hear the cheers!"

"I am not likely to forget them either," the Prince replied. "The rapture of the people was indescribable."

"Then what has gone wrong?"

"The liberated serfs believed the Tsar had made them a gift of the land. Now they are told that they have to pay their own regular taxes, so that although they are free men their poverty has increased."

"It cannot be true!" Lord Marston exclaimed.

"Unfortunately, it is," the Prince said. "Riots have broken out in many parts of the country and the peasants have even murdered land-owners and officials."

"I had heard there was some trouble," Lord Marston remarked, "but as you have so often said yourself, Ivan, Russia is a long way away."

As he spoke he remembered the Prince's background and his houses in which he had so often stayed.

It was to conjure up such a very different way of life from his own in England, so that sometimes he thought he had imagined the vast Estates, the thousands of serfs bowing to the ground before their master, and the barbaric splendour of the Prince's home which was muffled in heavy snow for many months of the year.

It had seemed to him as a boy almost a Kingdom on its own.

There had been enormous buildings, like a city belonging to one man, Winter Gardens where life-sized marble statues stood among a jungle of tropical plants, and, to emphasize the extravagance of it all, floors of tessellated marble, quartz, or lapis lazuli from the Siberian mines.

Lord Marston had only to shut his eyes to see rooms painted in green, dark blue, or crimson, filled with fantastic treasures, and to hear the crackling of the tall porcelain stoves which glowed by day and night.

They were fed by logs brought in by relays of bare-footed serfs who also tended the lamps and lit the hundreds of wax candles that burnt all over the house in occupied and unoccupied rooms alike.

Samovars, ikons, vodka, caviar, violins, wild horses, and even wilder riders were all part of the Prince's background.

It was all, Lord Marston had always thought, divorced from reality, and yet the magnificence of it did not detract from the personality of its owner.

Extravagance was not a word the Russian aristocrats understood.

An inamorata of a Grand Duke would travel in a sleigh festooned with emeralds, and Parma violets would be rushed from Grasse to prove the Ducal affection was undiminished.

Life was easily expendable: duelling was as frequent as games of cards, and crazy feats of daring were attempted for a wager or for sheer devilry.

Prince Ivan strode through the great rooms of his houses in the same way as he rode recklessly over the endless steppes, bringing to everything his own vivacious, exotic charm.

The only cloud in a sunlit sky where the Prince was concerned was women.

He had of course an irresistible attraction for them, but, while he was often infatuated and hunted them as another man might hunt with cunning and expertise a wild animal, once they were captured he was bored.

It was the chase which delighted him, not the kill, and no sooner had a woman surrendered herself abjectly and completely to his demands than he was looking over her shoulder for another amatory adventure.

"I may inform you," Lord Marston said now, "that I am here officially, and you are not to involve me in any scandal. Otherwise I shall be severely rapped over the knuckles, as I have been before."

"We will behave with the utmost circumspection," the Prince promised in his deep, attractive voice, but his eyes were dancing and Lord Marston looking at him exclaimed:

"Oh, Ivan, Ivan! You always get me into trouble!"

"If I did not, you would become disgustingly stiff-necked and insular," the Prince answered. "Well, I have told you about Russia. What is new in Paris?"

"Everything you can possibly imagine," Lord Marston replied. "Do you wish to see the Exhibition?"

"Good God! What is the reason for it?"

"Mostly political," Lord Marston answered. "The French became very apprehensive after Prussia defeated Austria at the Battle of Sadown last year!"

"What has that to do with an Exhibition?" the Prince asked.

"The French Army is in no condition to undertake a campaign against Prussia, so the Emperor, Napoleon III, has decided he must keep Parisian goodwill by providing them with magnificent jubilee shows and Court pageants."

Prince Ivan laughed.

"Pagan weapons," he said scornfully.

"Exactly," his friend agreed.

"I intend to ignore both the Exhibition and the Court," the Prince announced. "What else can you offer me?"

"The *demi-monde*."

"A female of the half-world?"

The Prince raised his eye-brows.

"Is this another word for courtesans, *les expertes ès Sciences, les femmes galaules, les grandes cocottes?*"

"Exactly," Lord Marston answered. "It was invented some years ago by Dumas to describe the world of the *déclassés*. You must have heard of his play?"

"I suppose so, but I have forgotten about it," the Prince answered.

"Then I will explain," Lord Marston went on. "In the second act the hero explains the *demi-monde* to another man. He compares certain women to a basket of peaches where each fruit has a tiny flaw, and he says:

" 'All the women round you have a fault in their past, a stain on their name. They have the same origins as Society women, they have the same appearance and prejudices, but they no longer belong to Society. They form what we call the *demi-mondaines*.' "

"It is an excellent description," the Prince said. "And let us, my dear Hugo, go and seek them out.

I suppose La Paiva is still walking about wearing a King's ransom in jewels?"

"Of course," Lord Marston replied.

La Paiva, who usually displayed two million francs worth of diamonds, pearls, and precious stones on her exquisite body, was considered the great *débauchée* of the century.

In an age of parvenues she remained the most immoral of them.

She was supposed to have no heart, but Lord Marston knew that where the Prince was concerned she had a soft spot which none of the other men who squandered fortunes upon her had been able to discover.

"What about *la Castiglione?*" the Prince enquired.

"The *Comtesse* is still the mistress of the Emperor, and another of your *chères amies,* Madame Mustard, has acquired an enormous fortune from the King of the Netherlands, who is crazily infatuated with her."

"A pretty piece," the Prince remarked laconically.

"You can see her and all the rest in the Bois and their usual haunts," Lord Marston said. "They continue to run through some wretched man's entire fortune in a matter of weeks, then throw him away like a sucked orange."

"I always come here expecting Paris to be different," the Prince said, "but it is invariably the same."

"Paris is *toujours* Paris," Lord Marston laughed, "and not even you, Ivan, can change that."

"I do not really think I want to," the Prince said, but he sounded doubtful.

His friend looked at him, then he asked:

"What are you looking for, Ivan? Ever since we have known each other I have always felt that you were searching for something."

The Prince smiled.

"You are becoming like my beloved mother, who, before she died last year, told me that if I fell in love with a 'good woman' it would be the saving of me."

"Did the Princess really say that?"

"She said it not once but a thousand times," the Prince answered. "She was obsessed by the idea that I should marry, settle down, and have a large family. Of course, I am not wholly averse to the idea, it is only that . . ."

He paused.

"You are afraid you would find it a dead bore?" Lord Marston finished.

"With the women I have known so far—yes!" the Prince answered.

He rose to his feet to walk across the Savonnerie carpet restlessly.

"The truth is, Hugo," he said, and his voice was serious, "I am well aware that I should take a wife and breed sons to inherit my vast possessions, but . . ."

He paused and Lord Marston did not speak but waited.

"I have a feeling," the Prince went on in a low voice, "that I am either an idealist or a romantic."

"You are both," his friend replied. "You always have been. Do you remember when we used to plan our lives together? I thought then, Ivan, that you always saw yourself as a benevolent despot bringing happiness to those who served you and living in some mythical, idealistic world."

"Dammit!" the Prince exclaimed. "You make me sound half-witted, but I suppose there is some truth in what you say. I want something, Hugo, I want it with all my heart, but I do not know what it is."

Lord Marston looked at him with understanding.

He was closer to the Prince than anyone else had ever been, and he knew how underneath his often flamboyant behaviour he was, as he wished to be, a generous and kind despot.

No serfs were better treated than those who had belonged to him, and long before the Tsar's Manifesto had given them their freedom there was no agitation for it on the Volkonski estates.

And in his private life the Prince was extremely open-handed.

No woman who left his arms could ever complain that he had not loaded her with presents and in many cases seen to it that her future was secure.

But whether the women were of the aristocratic *monde* or of the *demi-monde,* they always eventually ceased to hold the Prince and he was off again, galloping, as it were, towards an indefinable horizon in search of someone else.

With a quick change of mood he said:

"Curse it, I have not come to Paris to sermonise! For God's sake, Hugo, offer me a drink."

"My dear fellow, I am sorry!" Lord Marston exclaimed, "I was so astonished by your unexpected appearance that I forgot my manners."

He rose to ring the bell as he spoke and a few minutes later flunkeys carried in a bottle of champagne resting in a silver wine-cooler, and a tray on which there were not only glasses but also caviar, pâté de foie gras, and other delicacies.

The Prince sipped his champagne and remarked:

"You seem very comfortable here, but if you prefer to stay with me you know I shall be delighted."

"It is an idea," Lord Marston replied, "but I would not wish to offend the Ambassador and his charming wife. They have been exceptionally kind to me."

The Earl Cowley had been British Ambassador to Paris for fifteen years. He was polished, conscientious, and cautious, but it was his wife who represented Britain better than anyone else.

An experienced hostess, she was extremely popular with the French and had a great sense of humour.

Lord Marston related how she had become on practical-joke terms with the French Foreign Minister—Dromyn de Lhuys.

"When the Countess advertised for a wet-nurse

for her pregnant daughter, the Foreign Minister ap-
plied for the job, dressed up for the part by stuffing
himself with cushions."

The Prince laughed.

"That is worthy of some of our pranks, Hugo."

"I thought it would amuse you," Lord Marston said.
"But if you are going to behave outrageously, Ivan, I
had better move to that mansion of yours in the
Champs Élysées."

"Yes, do that," the Prince begged. "I intend to
give some very unusual parties."

Lord Marston held up his hands.

"For heaven's sake, Ivan, I know only too well
what your parties are like, and my reputation in Paris
will be completely ruined!"

"Nonsense!" the Prince retorted. "You know as well
as I do that I shall liven the whole place up."

That, Lord Marston thought, was an understate-
ment.

The Prince's parties in the past had been the talk
of Paris from the Court at the Tuileries Palace to
the lowest café on the Boulevards.

They were not only spectacles of wild extravagance,
they were also undoubtedly so amusing that those who
were not invited were humiliated to the point where
they would rather leave Paris, pretending they had
pressing engagements in the country, than admit that
their names had been omitted.

The two friends were still chatting when the door
opened and the British Ambassador entered.

Both men rose to their feet and after a speculative
glance at the Prince the Earl held out his hand.

"I am delighted to see Your Highness," he said.
"It has been too long since you paid us a visit."

"Your Excellency is very kind," the Prince answered, "but I am here alone, and I hope you will
forgive me if I steal your guest from you to keep
me company."

The Earl looked at Lord Marston with a smile.

"I think you have sent back enough reports by now to fill the Prime Minister's waste-paper basket. It is time you enjoyed yourself."

"Thank you, My Lord," Lord Marston replied.

* * *

The Prince's open chaise drawn by two outstanding horses was waiting in the Embassy yard.

An hour later the two friends drove off together after Lord Marston had left instructions for his valet to pack and follow him to the Prince's mansion.

"Now, what shall we do tonight?" the Prince asked.

"I will take you to see something new," Lord Marston replied, "which I think will interest you."

"What is that?"

"I am not going to tell you, it shall be a surprise."

"Very well," the Prince answered, "but I insist on a good dinner first."

"Magnys or Véfour?" Lord Marston enquired.

"Véfour," the Prince said promptly. "I want to eat and not be distracted by all the celebrated diners who will ornament Magnys."

Lord Marston smiled.

"Very well," he said. "We will have their *spécialité*, which I know was one of your favourite dishes in the past."

He was thinking as he spoke of the fine Rhenish carp which had been declared by Alfred Delvau in *Les Plaisirs de Paris*, which had just been published, to be one of the glories of the place.

Delvau was the same author who had said:

"Pleasure is the mania of Paris, their malady and their weakness. They love violent emotions and entertainments which create noise, stir, and excitement."

It was a description, Lord Marston thought, which might also apply to the Prince.

Nevertheless, after some weeks of attending nothing but Court and Embassy functions and playing the part of the perfect diplomat, he felt now a quickening of his pulse.

The two men were welcomed at the Véfour. The restaurant was in the Palais Royal, which during the reign of Louis XVI the *Duc* d'Orleans had turned into a place of gambling and amusement, and he had become overnight one of the richest men in France.

It was still the haunt of *les cocottes,* who had made it their special promenade, and Véfour was decorated in the same way as it had been immediately after the Revolution.

With its red plush sofas and its mirrors inset in painted wooden panels it was comfortable, intimate, and appropriate for those who wished to concentrate on what they were eating.

The Prince and Lord Marston ordered carefully and selectively.

The *maître d'hôtel* suggested a "Russian bird" and the Prince looked surprised until Lord Marston explained:

"There is now a large trade between Paris and Russia in game. The birds are packed in oats and put in wicker baskets, and arrive here in five days."

"Such is progress!" the Prince remarked ironically.

"Alternatively, you can have birds'-nests from China, ortali from Italy, or truffles from Périgord," Lord Marston joked.

"In France I expect snails," the Prince said firmly, and ordered them.

Then as they waited for their food to be brought to them they sat back comfortably, sipping champagne and talking.

As so often when they were alone, they discussed subjects which would have surprised many of their friends: philosophy, literature, politics, arguing with each other and capping each other's quotations, being in fact both of them exceedingly erudite.

When dinner was finished the Prince's mood changed with a swiftness that was characteristic of him.

"Now, Hugo," he asked, "where are you taking me?"

"Hold your breath," Lord Marston replied. "To see *Cinderella!*"

"*Cinderella?*" the Prince exclaimed.

"At the Théâtre Impérial du Châtelet."

"I am too old for fairy-tales!" the Prince exclaimed.

"Not for this one," his friend said firmly.

"I warn you, I shall walk out if I am bored."

"I am prepared to bet quite a considerable sum that you will not be."

"Very well," the Prince said in a resigned tone.

They left Véfour and walked a little way down a narrow pavement to where the Prince's carriage was waiting.

It was a closed barouche with two men on the box and very comfortable inside.

There was a sable rug in case the evening grew cold, but for the moment the April air was warm and mellow.

The two friends crossed their legs and puffed reflectively on their long cigars.

They drove through the Boulevards with their brightly lit cafés, the crowds perambulating up and down in the golden light from the gas-lamps.

Outside the Theatre there was, although the performance had started over an hour before, a considerable crowd standing about blocking the doorways and quite a number still trying to get seats.

"Has Paris returned to its childhood?" the Prince asked ironically.

"This is a fairy-story with a difference," Lord Marston explained. "It has five acts and thirty scenes."

The Prince groaned.

"Lavish production is a feature of the contemporary Theatre," Lord Marston said in the tone of one giving a lecture. "You will see the Green Grotto, the Fiery Mountain, the Azure Lake, the Glowworms' Palace, and the Golden Clouds."

Again the Prince groaned, but Lord Marston thought that he was nevertheless somewhat intrigued.

They arrived during the first intermission. There was a crowd of men in the auditorium attempting to get drinks, and the clamour and the hum of voices was deafening.

The lights were up in the house; tall jets of gas illuminated a great crystal pendant with a stream of yellow and rose which was reflected from the arched dome to the pit in a deluge of light.

The footlights threw a sharp flood of colour on the purple draperies of the curtain, and in the boxes men with opera-glasses and women with lorgnettes were contemplating one another.

Lord Marston had taken the precaution of engaging the largest box, which was known as the Royal Box, for his friend.

As they entered it, young gentlemen standing in the stalls with low-cut waist-coats and gardenias in their button-holes turned their opera-glasses on them.

There was a flutter of hands from many of the other boxes and the Prince bowed first to one, then to another of the ladies who recognised him.

"You will be deluged with invitations tomorrow," Lord Marston remarked.

The Prince ran an appraising eye round the Theatre.

"I promise you, Hugo, I shall be very selective."

The intermission bell was ringing and now the audience were returning to their seats.

There was the usual confusion of people who had seated themselves being obliged to rise again, and the conductor of the Orchestra took his place. The sound of conversation grew lower and quieter although occasionally it was broken by coarse voices.

They had reached the part of the play, Lord Marston realised, where the scene was a Fiery Mountain.

Gnomes were busy working under iridescent rocks bathed in a red light that was more vivid than rubies.

Then the waves of the Azure Lake grew larger and the ruby fire from the mountain was extinguished by cool blue lights in which half-naked nymphs were swimming.

It was so fantastic that the whole audience burst into applause and for a moment even the Prince seemed impressed.

After a chorus from the gnomes and a song from Prince Charming, who was looking for Cinderella, the scene dissolved into darkness and there was a "knock-about" turn between two comedians whose broad innuendos had the whole place in convulsions.

The Prince's attention was waning.

He was looking at the occupants of the other boxes, doubtless, Lord Marston thought, considering if there was anyone present with whom he wished to renew an acquaintance.

Then as the comedians went off there was a sudden hush and the house was in darkness. The Orchestra began very softly a classical tune which was different from anything they had heard previously.

"This is what I brought you to see," Lord Marston said.

The Prince with a somewhat questioning expression on his face turned his head towards the stage.

The curtains were drawn back and now instead of the gaudy and flamboyant colours which had characterised the décor for all the other scenes there were only curtains which seemed to melt into the shadows.

Onto the stage came a dancer.

She was not in the least like any dancer the Prince had ever seen before.

Used to the Imperial Russian Ballet with their blocked ballet-shoes, short frilled tutus, low-cut bodices, and accentuated make-up, he saw in this girl a complete contrast.

She wore a Grecian robe of white silk, and her hair was loose but drawn back from her face and caught in a style that was neither classical nor modern.

She had sandals on her feet and wore no ornamentation of any sort, nor as far as the audience could see did she wear any cosmetics.

She stood for a moment quite still in the centre of the stage, then she began to dance.

It was a dance and at the same time a mime which told a story which was simple and so brilliantly portrayed that no-one could fail to understand.

She was a child, happy and carefree, thrilled with the flowers, the butterflies, the birds, and as her arms went out towards them one could almost see the birds fluttering above her and the butterflies hovering over the flowers.

It was a dance so exquisite in every movement, in every gesture, that the audience seemed to hold its breath and there was not a sound in the whole auditorium.

She was joy, she was youth, she believed that God was in His Heaven and all was right with the world.

She was everything that anyone remembered of his childhood, she was innocence, she was beauty itself, and it almost seemed as if she held both happiness and beauty in her arms.

The curtain came down and for a moment there was that silence which every actor and actress knows marks the summit of real appreciation.

Then the applause broke out thunderously, seeming to shake the very Theatre itself.

"She is fantastic!" the Prince exclaimed. "Who is she?"

"Her name is Lokita," Lord Marston replied.

The audience was silent again, and the music had begun, but now it was very different, sombre and throbbing with grief.

The curtains were drawn back, the décor was unchanged, and Lokita once again was standing in the centre of the stage.

She wore a black cloak and there was a wreath of flowers in her hand.

She just stood there, and yet there was something in her pose that made a lump come into the throat of everyone who watched her.

She moved forward, laid the wreath on the grave of someone she had loved, and looked down at it, and it was obvious that her heart was breaking.

She had lost what was irreplaceable, she had lost a part of herself; it was almost as if she too lay in the grave, no longer a part of the world that lived.

She wept and the women in the audience wept with her; she reached out yearning arms as if to draw back to life the person who had left her. Then in despair she sank lower and lower, her misery overwhelming her to the point when she too longed to die.

Then suddenly in the sound of the music there was a note of hope, a note which made her first raise her tear-stained face, then slowly, so slowly that it was almost an agony of apprehension to watch her, she rose to her feet.

It was there above her, near her, enveloping her, the knowledge that there is no death but life.

Gradually it percolated through her mind, her spirit, her soul.

Suddenly she was fully aware that it was the truth, there was no death! She had not lost the one she loved.

Now there was light, there was faith! She flung off her cloak and danced as she had before—danced with happiness. And not alone.

One could almost see the person beside her to whom she spoke, to whom she clung. They were together and there was no longer grief and despair but a joy and a rapture that were part of the Divine.

The curtain fell, and now there was a sigh that seemed to come from everybody's lips, a sigh that a human being makes after he has been transported into a world of wonder and delight.

"Good God!"

The exclamation came involuntarily from the Prince's lips.

Then like everyone else he was clapping, applauding, his eyes on the curtain, waiting for the dancer to reappear and take her bows.

"You will not see her again," Lord Marston said quietly.

The Prince looked at him in surprise.

"She does not take curtain-calls? Why ever not?"

"I do not know—the audience break their hands and crash their voices, but she pays no attention."

The Prince was astonished. He had never heard of any dancer, singer, or actress who did not enjoy a heady quantity of applause.

Then as the curtain drew back to reveal another flamboyant, colourful décor, he said:

"I must meet her. Let us go round backstage."

"It is quite useless. She will see no-one."

"Rubbish!" the Prince replied. "She will see me. Call a servant."

As he spoke he drew a card from his pocket and wrote a sentence on the back of it.

Lord Marston watched him with an amused smile, then beckoned to one of the attendants.

The Prince held out the card to him.

"Take this to *Mademoiselle* Lokita," he said, "and bring me an answer."

He gave the man a louis as he spoke, but the attendant shook his head.

"C'est impossible, Monsieur!"

"Nothing is impossible," the Prince replied. "I wish the *Mademoiselle* to have supper with me. As you will see by my card, I am Prince Ivan Volkonski."

"I am sorry, *Monsieur le Prince,* but *M'mselle* Lokita will have supper with no-one."

He glanced towards the stage.

"In fact, *Monsieur,* by this time she will have left the Theatre."

"Left the Theatre?" the Prince asked sharply. "She does not appear in the finale?"

"*Non, Monsieur, M'mselle* Lokita speaks to no-one. As soon as her performance is finished she departs."

The Prince waved the man away and said to Lord Marston:

"Is he speaking the truth?"

"So I have been told," Lord Marston replied. "Lokita is a sensation. She has been written up in all the newspapers, but she refuses to give interviews and it is known that she is never seen in public."

"She is fantastic! Stupendous!" the Prince exclaimed. "I thought I was an expert on dancing, but this is different from anything I have seen before."

"That is what I thought you would say," Lord Marston said with a smile. "The rest of the show is banal. Shall we leave?"

"No, dammit! I have no intention of leaving," the Prince said. "We will go behind and I will find out if you are telling me the truth."

"Very well," Lord Marston agreed, "but I can assure you you are wasting your time."

The Prince did not listen to him, but led the way from the box and round to the stage-door with the air of a man to whom it was all very familiar.

Behind the scenes there was the usual confusion of ropes and canvas, of scene-shifters swearing at those who got in their way and actors hurrying to get back to their dressing-rooms.

There were flowers being brought in from the street in baskets or arranged in bouquets ornamented with long streamers of satin ribbons.

As they passed these, Lord Marston saw that a great number of them were for Lokita.

On the thick, overheated atmosphere there was a strong smell characteristic of every Theatre back-stage: the stink of gas, the glue used on the canvas of the scenery, the filth of dark corners, the sharp tang of toilet-waters, and the scent of soap from the dressing-rooms, all of which seemed to mingle with a dozen different perfumes.

As the two men walked along a narrow passage they heard the noise of washing-basins, the laughter of women calling to one another, and the racket of doors continually banging.

The Prince had found the Stage-door Keeper in his box and was asking him the way to Lokita's dressing-room.

"You can go there if it pleases you, *Monsieur*," the man was saying, brought into a good humour by the number of louis which the Prince had pressed into his palm, "but *M'mselle*'s not there."

"Where is she?" the Prince asked almost fiercely.

"She's left! *M'mselle* Lokita always leaves the Theatre, *Monsieur,* as soon as her act is over."

"Why does she do that?"

The man shrugged his shoulders.

"How should I know? *M'mselle* does not confide in me!"

"There is a gentleman who waits for her, perhaps? Who escorts her when she leaves?"

The Stage-door Keeper shook his head.

"Non, M'mselle Lokita leaves only with *Madame,* who is always in attendance on her."

"What is *Madame*'s name?"

The man thought for a moment, then mispronouncing it he said:

"An-der-son."

"That is English!" the Prince exclaimed. "Is it not, Hugo?"

"It sounds like it," Lord Marston agreed.

"Now listen to me," the Prince said. "I wish to meet *Mademoiselle* Lokita. If I leave a note here, will you see that she receives it tomorrow?"

"I can give to to *Madame* Anderson," the man said doubtfully.

"It will be for *Mademoiselle* Lokita!"

Again the man shrugged his shoulders.

"It is *Madame* Anderson who sees to everything. As I said, *Monsieur*, the little one does not speak. She just goes to her dressing-room in silence. In silence she walks on the stage, in silence she leaves."

"I do not believe it!" the Prince said in an exasperated tone as he and Lord Marston drove away.

"That is what quite a number of people have said already," Lord Marston replied, "but you had to find out for yourself."

"I *have* to meet her!"

"I doubt if it will be possible, but you can but try. Anyway, you have to admit she is unique."

"Of course she is! Unique, original, sensational! But where does that get me?"

Lord Marston laughed.

"Exactly where you are now—frustrated and at the same time, you must admit, Ivan, vastly intrigued!"

"Of course I am," the Prince agreed, "but I can assure you, Hugo, that is not enough. I intend to find out a great deal more, and nothing and no-one will stop me from becoming acquainted with Lokita."

Lord Marston lay back in the carriage and laughed.

"I like to watch you when you are tracking down a prey, Ivan, but I have a feeling, although I may be wrong, that this time you will hunt in vain."

"God in Heaven!" the Prince remarked. "If any other man had said that to me I would call him a liar, but where you are concerned, Hugo, it is a challenge! How much do you bet that I do not succeed where all others have failed?"

Lord Marston considered for a moment.

"I am not going to wager you in money, Ivan. That would be too easy for you. But I have a new hunter, a grey which I consider to be superlative. He has an Arab strain in him, of course, but it is his training that has been so exceptional."

"Well?" the Prince asked with a smile.

Lord Marston said slowly:

"I will wager Kingfisher against one of your finest stallions!"

"I accept!" the Prince said. "If we ride tomorrow morning you shall have a look at Suliman. He is a magnificent beast and he cost me more than any other horse I have ever bought. What is more, I intend to keep him!"

"I shall enjoy riding him in Rotten Row," Lord Marston said confidently.

"I am wondering how Lokita will look on Kingfisher!" the Prince retorted.

Both men laughed, then the Prince said:

"She is not English, whatever nationality her *Duenna* may be—I would stake my life on that!"

"I agree with you there," Lord Marston replied, "and yet her hair is fair."

"But her eyes are dark," the Prince said. "It is strange they should be dark when she has fair hair, and yet I would swear it was absolutely natural."

"It could be nothing else," Lord Marston said simply.

"How could she have learnt to dance like that? There is no school that I know of in the whole world that teaches that type of dancing."

"You are asking the same question that every newspaper in Paris has asked. They have gone into rhapsodies over her, and yet for the first time even the most ferrety reporter has found absolutely nothing to relate personally."

Lord Marston paused to add slowly:

"They do not know where she comes from, where she lives, what language she speaks, or anything whatever about her!"

"It is unbelievable!" the Prince exclaimed. "If you had told me that about any dancer in any country I would not have believed you."

"Exactly what I felt myself," Lord Marston agreed. "I have been to see Lokita four times and each time I have come away astonished that in this sophisticated city, which is a triumph of artificiality, there is something so fundamentally pure that one watches her with one's heart rather than with one's eyes."

"That is what I felt myself," the Prince said in a low voice, "but it was more than that, Hugo. That girl spoke to my soul, and I swear to you it is something which has never happened to me before!"

Chapter Two

The applause vibrated round the auditorium. Men and women were on their feet shouting and clapping.

The noise was thunderous and as Lokita walked into the wings the Stage Manager rushed forward.

"Take a curtain-call, *M'mselle*—for God's sake, take a call! They are tearing the place apart!"

Before Lokita could reply, Miss Anderson's voice came sharply:

"Certainly not! You know it is part of *Mademoiselle*'s contract that she should not take curtain-calls."

As she spoke she wrapped a woollen shawl round Lokita's shoulders and drew her away down the passage which led to the dressing-rooms.

"Mon Dieu! C'est incroyable!" the Stage Manager muttered, and hurriedly signalled to the Orchestra to play something noisy to calm the excited audience.

Lokita and Miss Anderson climbed the iron stairs to the dressing-room she had been allotted on the first *étage*.

It was a small square room with a very low ceiling draped with a light brown cloth. Curtains of the same material hanging from a copper rod made a separate compartment at one end.

The window, which opened onto a small court-yard,

24

looked onto a blank, crumbling wall against which the lights from the dressing-room threw yellow squares in the black of the night.

The room was redolent with the fragrance of flowers which stood everywhere, on the floor, on the dressing-table, on the chairs.

There were baskets, bouquets, garlands, all carrying the cards of their donors and all betraying an extravagance that was characteristic in Paris.

As Miss Anderson shut the door behind Lokita she said:

"You were very good tonight, my dear."

Lokita gave a little sigh almost as if she awoke from a dream.

"I felt Papa near me," she said, "and I thought that he was pleased with me."

Miss Anderson knew it was through her conviction of this that she had mesmerised the audience and left hardly a dry eye in the whole Theatre.

But she had no wish to make Lokita feel self-conscious about what she had portrayed on the stage, and she was aware that the secret of her success lay in the fact that immersed in her own imagination she danced what she felt.

Aloud she said simply:

"I am sure your father would have been very proud of you."

"I hope so," Lokita said with a little catch in her breath. "He was closer to me tonight than he has ever been before."

She moved through the forest of flowers behind the curtain to take off her Grecian robe and slip into the clothes that were hanging there.

There was a knock on the door.

"Who is it?" Miss Anderson asked sharply.

"More flowers for *M'mselle* Lokita!" the page-boy answered.

She opened the door, took a basket from him, and

put it down on the only space available, which was in the centre of the dressing-table.

He waited and she knew that he expected to be tipped. She handed him some small coins and after he had thanked her he walked away whistling.

"More flowers?" Lokita asked.

Miss Anderson glanced at the basket that she had just set down.

"White orchids."

"How lovely!"

Lokita came from behind the curtain, tying the sash she wore round the tiny waist of her plain white gown, which had only a suspicion of a bustle at the back.

"Star orchids!" she exclaimed. "Andy, they are beautiful!"

"You have plenty of flowers at home," Miss Anderson said. "These can go with the rest to the Hospital."

"No, I think I would like to keep these," Lokita said. "They are so beautiful, more beautiful than anything else I have ever been given."

The basket certainly seemed unique. There was something fragile and classical about it, unlike the flamboyant offerings that stood about the dressing-room.

Most of these were decorated with huge bows of satin ribbon and in contrast to the delicacy of the white orchids they seemed garish and vulgar.

"I shall take these home with me," Lokita decided. "I wonder who has sent them."

She looked into the centre of the basket as she spoke, then gave a little exclamation.

"There is something else here, Andy!"

"What is it?" Miss Anderson asked.

Lokita drew out a small white velvet box. Beside it was a card and as she handed the box to Miss Anderson she read aloud:

"Prince Ivan Volkonski."

Miss Anderson made an exclamation that was half

a cry, and at the same time she opened the jewel-box.

Inside was a butterfly set in blue-white diamonds!

There was no need to read the name on the box to know that it had come from Oscar Massin, who created jewellery which could compare with the finest work of the eighteenth century.

His jewel, Lilac Blossom, which had been bought by the Empress and was on show at the Exhibition, was a triumph of the jeweller's art.

Massin was famous for his jewelled flowers and ears of corn, and only the previous week Lokita had admired in his window a spray of lilies-of-the-valley which had seemed to shine with an iridescent light.

Miss Anderson stood staring at the butterfly which glittered in the gas-lights in the dressing-room and seemed almost to flutter.

"It really is beautiful!" Lokita said, looking at it too.

Miss Anderson shut the case with a snap.

"And an insult!" she said harshly.

Lokita raised her eyes and there was a question in them.

She had very expressive eyes of deep green, their emerald hue flecked with gold.

Her dark lashes gave them a mystery that made them at times seem to hold the secrets of a forest pool.

"An insult!" Miss Anderson repeated.

"Perhaps the Prince did not mean it to be one," Lokita said softly.

"I know exactly what he meant," Miss Anderson replied grimly. "Put on your cloak. Pull the hood right over your face. We must leave immediately!"

She spoke so commandingly that Lokita obeyed, putting on an enveloping cloak of deep blue velvet and pulling the hood over her face as she had been told, so that she was practically unidentifiable.

As they left the dressing-room she gave one last look at the star orchids standing on the table, and only as she went down the passage did she realise that she still held in her hand the card with the Prince's name on it.

Miss Anderson went ahead down the iron staircase and along the corridor crowded with actors and actresses moving towards the stage in readiness for the next act.

The girls were laughing and giggling together and the men were fidgeting with their elaborate costumes and their wigs.

From the front of the House came the sound of the Orchestra playing stridently, and inevitably there were the raised voices of two people snarling at each other and losing their tempers over some incident which had happened on stage.

Miss Anderson pushed her way through with Lokita just behind her and they reached the comparative quiet of the stage-door.

Only as they did so did they see a tall, elegant man come in through the door.

He wore his top-hat at an angle on his dark head and a cloak lined with red satin swung from his shoulders.

In the button-hole of his evening-coat was not the usual gardenia that was the *dernier cri* amongst gentlemen of fashion, but a star-shaped orchid.

Miss Anderson turned back, seized Lokita by the arm, and pulled her into the shadow of a doorway.

"*Mademoiselle* Lokita is in her dressing-room?" they heard the gentleman ask.

He had a deep resonant voice, Lokita noticed, and she thought, peeping at him from the darkness, that he was the most magnificent man she had ever seen in her whole life.

Her father had been good-looking and she had always loved seeing him in evening-dress with his spotless white shirt and his tight-fitting long-tailed evening-coat.

But this stranger wore his clothes with an air that

was somehow regal, and she thought too that his face, though not English, was proud, aristocratic, and at the same time exceedingly attractive.

"You sent my flowers to *Mademoiselle?*" the Prince asked the Stage-door Keeper.

As he spoke there was the glimpse of a golden louis passing from hand to hand.

"They went upstairs a few minutes ago, *Monsieur le Prince.*"

Lokita gave a little start.

Now she knew who the stranger was! He was the Prince who had sent her the star-shaped orchids and also the diamond butterfly which Miss Anderson still held in her hand.

"Dressing-room twenty-nine, *Monsieur,*" the Stage-door Keeper said.

The Prince nodded an acknowledgement, then he turned and passed Lokita and Miss Anderson in the shadows without seeing them, walking swiftly down the now empty passage towards the iron staircase they had just descended.

No sooner was he out of sight than Miss Anderson walked to the box in which the Stage-door Keeper sat.

"When His Highness returns," she said in a voice of steel, "hand him this and tell him that *Mademoiselle* Lokita considers it an insult!"

She slapped the white velvet box down in front of the man as she spoke.

Then as Lokita opened her lips to protest she found herself hurried out through the stage-door and onto the pavement outside.

The gas-lamps revealed a long line of *fiacres* with their skinny horses waiting patiently for the performance to end.

Miss Anderson helped Lokita into the nearest one, gave the *cocher* the address, and they drove off without anyone observing their departure.

It was too early for the crowd of gentlemen who

waited for the Chorus-Girls or the stage-struck
women who wanted to see their idols off stage.

"I feel that was rather rude, Andy," Lokita said as
they drove away.

"One has to be rude to those sort of people."

"The Prince is very handsome."

"Which doubtless accounts for his reputation!" Miss
Anderson remarked sourly.

"You know about him, Andy?" Lokita asked. "Tell
me who he is. You know how interested I am in anything about Russia."

"There is good and bad in every country," Miss
Anderson replied, "and Prince Ivan Volkonski, thank
goodness, is not typical of Imperial Russia."

"He is important?"

"His family is. His mother was a Romanov."

"Then he is related to the Tsar!"

"A cousin, I believe, but that is no reason for you
to be interested in him. When it is less crowded than
it is at the moment, I will take you to see the Russian
Pavilion at the Exhibition."

"I am longing to do that," Lokita answered, "but
how long have we to wait?"

"The Exhibition was only opened on April first. At
the moment, according to the newspapers, it is
crowded to stupefaction. It will not be closed until
November. There is plenty of time for you to see everything without being torn to pieces."

There was a little silence, then Lokita said:

"Tell me more about Prince Ivan Volkonski."

"He is of no interest to you."

"But he is Russian! Oh, Andy, do you think I shall
ever meet any Russians, except of course dear Serge?"

Miss Anderson did not reply and after a moment
Lokita said:

"I want more books to read about St. Petersburg
and Moscow. It will be amusing now to see if I can
find the Volkonski name in them."

"I have told you—forget him," Miss Anderson said sharply.

"But why? Why?"

"Because I say so!"

Lokita laughed, and it was a very musical sound.

"Oh, Andy, you used to say that when I was a child. You forget I am now eighteen and grown up."

"All the more reason for me to take care of you," Miss Anderson replied.

Now there was a softness in her voice that had not been there before.

"You have always done that, Andy dear, and often I wonder what I would do without you."

She was not aware that in the expression on the face of the woman sitting beside her there was a fear which always lurked at the back of her mind. Aloud Miss Anderson said:

"Tomorrow after you have ridden in the Bois we might go driving outside Paris. I know you like being in the country."

Lokita was astute enough to realise that she was being offered a treat to take her mind off the Prince, but aloud she said:

"That would be lovely, Andy, but I think *Madame* Albertini is coming to give me a lesson."

"To my mind her lessons are a waste of time," Miss Anderson said, the sharp note back in her voice. "There is nothing more *Madame* can teach you, as both you and she are well aware."

"But we owe her so much. It was through her that I got this engagement in the Theatre and the enormous salary they are now paying me."

"Every time we go to that place it takes years off my life," Miss Anderson said as if she spoke to herself. "I cannot think what your father would have said if he knew."

"He does know," Lokita said very quietly, "and when I felt him near me tonight I was sure he understood."

She spoke with such complete conviction that Miss Anderson did not reply.

They drove in silence until, having passed up the Champs Élysées and travelled on for some distance, they came on the edge of the Bois to a small house set in a garden that was filled with trees.

It was small, grey, and so symmetrical with its wooden shutters that it looked like a doll's house.

Lokita stepped out and opening the iron gate ran up the minute drive which led to the front door.

Even as she reached it the door opened and an elderly maid with a starched white cap and apron stood waiting for her.

"It was a success, *M'mselle?*" she asked, smiling.

"A great success, Marie! I never heard the audience make such a noise!"

"The newspapers will sing your praises again tomorrow," Marie said with an unmistakable expression of admiration in her eyes.

Lokita, however, was not listening.

She took off her velvet cloak and laid it on a chair in the tiny hall, then walked into the Salon ahead of Miss Anderson, who stopped to speak to Marie.

Quickly, with her back to the door, Lokita slipped the Prince's card, which she still held in her hand, down the front of her gown.

She could feel the cardboard hard against her breasts and she wondered why she wished to keep it.

Then told herself it was because it was Russian, and anything to do with Russia was very close to her heart.

The Salon was fragrant with the scent of flowers. They were not the stiff, exotic, hot-house flowers that had filled her dressing-room, but flowers from the garden and from the countryside where she and Miss Anderson went for their drives.

As she moved across the room Lokita touched a blossom of white lilac which stood in a vase on a side-table, then bent her head to sniff its subtle perfume.

"You must be hungry," Miss Anderson said from

the doorway. "Marie is bringing supper into the Dining-Room."

Lokita turned around.

"I am coming, Andy," she replied, "but I am more thirsty than hungry."

As she moved across the room she felt the Prince's card and wondered what he had thought when he found that his white orchids had been left in her dressing-room and the butterfly on which he must have spent an enormous sum of money was waiting for him at the stage-door.

* * *

The Prince in dressing-room 29 looked at the flowers that filled it.

He thought for one moment that his star-shaped orchids were not among them, until he saw the basket standing on the dressing-table.

He had realised at a glance that it was too late and Lokita, despite what the Stage-door Keeper had said, had gone.

Through the half-open curtain he could see the white gown she had worn on the stage hanging from a rail and beneath it the very small pair of silver sandals which she had worn on her feet.

He had left his box the moment she had left the stage, but the crowds had prevented him from moving swiftly and he was sure now that he had only missed her by a few seconds.

The Prince had been in a great many dressing-rooms and it struck him that this one was somehow different from the others he had known.

For a moment he could not think what it was, since all dressing-rooms looked much the same.

Then he realised that the dressing-table did not contain the usual mixed assortment of scent-bottles, glass bottles of cosmetic oils, powders, rouge, and grease-paint, with which he was all too familiar.

There were no cuttings from the newspapers stuck on the side of the mirror or on the wall.

There were no good-luck charms, no hare's foot or chicken-bone or blessed medallion, nor were there the dolls with which many of the actresses adorned their dressing-rooms and their beds.

There was indeed nothing personal, the Prince saw, except a plain brush and beside it a comb.

He had been right, he thought, in thinking that Lokita used no cosmetics on her face, but he found it difficult to believe that any woman who was part of the theatre should have so few personal belongings.

It was then, as he stood staring at the dressing-table, that he looked at the basket of orchids he had sent her.

Even as Lokita had done, he thought the star-shaped blossoms he had chosen so carefully made every other flower in the place seem coarse and vulgar.

As he looked closer in the basket in which they were arranged, he realised that two things were missing: the white velvet box he had placed there himself and his visiting card.

"So she has taken it!"

There was a smile of satisfaction on his lips as he turned and walked down the iron staircase and back to the Stage-door Keeper.

"*Mademoiselle* Lokita was not there," he said.

"*Non, Monsieur,* she left a few seconds after you went in search of her. You must have passed her in the corridor."

"Impossible!" the Prince replied.

"*Madame* Anderson left this box for you, *Monsieur,*" the Stage-door Keeper said, pushing it forward as he spoke. "She said I was to tell you that *M'mselle* Lokita considered it an insult."

The Prince stiffened, then he picked up the jewel-box, put it in his pocket, and without another word walked out onto the street.

He had confidently expected that his gift, which, like

the flowers, he had chosen with discrimination, would have been accepted as all his gifts had been in the past.

He had wooed many actresses in his time, including several ballerinas of the Imperial Russian Ballet.

Just one or two of them had played "hard-to-get," but he had never met a woman who was not won over by diamonds if they were large and expensive enough.

To his surprise, the Prince found himself wondering as he drove away from the Theatre if his tactics had been at fault.

Lokita was obviously very different from any other actress, and perhaps in fact it had been an insult to offer anyone so exquisite and so ethereal a present which was material and mundane.

"I should have been more subtle," he told himself.

He was still frowning as he walked into the Café Anglais, where he had arranged to meet Lord Marston.

They had agreed that if, as the Prince confidently expected, Lokita came out to supper with him, he would make himself scarce; but now there was a smile of amusement on Lord Marston's face as the Prince sat down at his table.

"I gather she refused to have supper with you?" he remarked.

"She had left the Theatre before I could reach her," the Prince replied crossly.

"Without thanking you for such an expensive *bijou?*"

"It was returned by her *Duenna* saying that *Mademoiselle* Lokita considered it an insult."

Lord Marston was obviously delighted.

"I warned you not to treat her as if she were an ordinary Chorus-Girl to be dazzled by the flutter of gems."

"You were right, Hugo," the Prince said ruefully. "Now I shall have to start again."

"You might just as well acknowledge defeat, my

dear fellow. Better men than you have knocked on that door without avail."

"Better men than me? Dammit! What do you mean by that?" the Prince asked truculently.

Lord Marston laughed.

"Ivan, that I should ever live to see the day when a woman on whom you had set your heart did not fall into your arms like an over-ripe peach!"

"You wait!" the Prince said. "This is only the beginning! I shall succeed in the end, and then you will hand over Kingfisher with a good grace."

"I will be riding him for a long time yet," Lord Marston said boastfully.

"That remains to be seen," the Prince replied. "What the hell are we going to do this evening, then?"

They visited two parties given by women who considered themselves to be members of *la Garde,* the top *demi-mondaines* before whom the gentlemen of Paris bowed as to some heathen goddess.

It was quite obvious to Lord Marston that his friend was bored and they went on to one of the *Maisons de Plaisir,* where the *Madame* greeted them effusively and the most alluring and expressive *cocottes* were paraded for their inspection.

The Prince clearly was becoming more and more bored, and finally they drove home to his house in the Champs Élysées.

"It is quite early for you," Lord Marston said, "in fact it is only three o'clock."

"I am not going to bed."

Lord Marston looked surprised.

"Then what are you going to do?" he asked.

"I am going riding," the Prince replied.

Ten minutes later he was trotting up the Champs Élysées to put his horse into a wild gallop once he had reached the Bois.

Lord Marston did not accompany him.

He knew only too well that when his friend was either upset or thinking out some outrageous plan, the only way he could find relief from his own emotions was to ride.

"He will feel better in the morning," Lord Marston said to himself and retired to bed.

He was awakened by the Prince coming into his room soon after dawn and he was still in riding-clothes.

He did not look tired but somehow intensely alive and elated, as if he had solved a problem and was thereby exhilarated.

"Go away, Ivan!" Lord Marston protested. "You look disgustingly fit and I hate being woken so early."

"You are getting old and staid, Hugo," the Prince replied. "I will leave you to your slumbers, but there is one question I wish to ask you."

"What is that?" Lord Marston asked drowsily.

"Our wager," the Prince said. "Does it count if Lokita acquiesces in my demands—unwillingly?"

Lord Marston sat up in bed.

"Ivan, what are you planning? I do not like the sound of it!"

"I asked you a question and I want an answer."

"Did you say—unwillingly?" Lord Marston enquired. "What can you mean by that? You can hardly hand-cuff the girl and drag her out to supper with you."

He looked at the Prince as he spoke and saw a sudden glitter in his eyes.

"Whatever you are thinking of doing, forget it!" he said sharply. "And if you are thinking about our wager—no! She has supper with you, or any other meal you like, because she has accepted you as a companion."

"That is all I wanted to know," the Prince answered.

He walked towards the door but Lord Marston, now fully awake, put out his hands as if to stop him.

"Ivan, behave yourself!" he commanded. "You are in Paris now and you cannot exercise your barbaric Russian ideas in a civilised community without evoking very unpleasant repercussions."

"Who said I intended to be barbaric?" the Prince asked.

There was something ingenuous about his voice which did not deceive his friend.

"I do not know what you are planning," Lord Marston said, "but I bet one hundred thousand francs that it is the sort of thing which will involve you—and me—in a lot of trouble. Do try to remember, Ivan, that I am here as a representative of the British Government!"

"You can always return to the Embassy," the Prince suggested mockingly.

"And leave you to your own nefarious devices?" Lord Marston questioned. "I shall do nothing of the sort! I shall try to be a restraining influence on you."

"An aim in which you have always failed ever since we have known each other," the Prince remarked.

Lord Marston had to admit that this was all too true, but he said earnestly:

"Be careful, Ivan, that you do not go too far. You say yourself that St. Petersburg is barred to you at the moment. That leaves only Paris and London, and if you do anything really outrageous you will be turned out of those Capitals as well."

The Prince did not reply and Lord Marston looked at him apprehensively.

"Apart from anything else," he said in a different tone, "I thought last night, when Lokita was dancing, that it would be a pity if she was spoilt by you or anyone else. She is unique, perfect and untouched, like a flower."

"I have to meet her," the Prince said.

"But why?" Lord Marston enquired. "There are millions of other women in the world."

The Prince walked across the room to open a window farther than it was already.

"Have you ever felt, Hugo, that you were being carried along by fate?"

"Are you really asking me such a question?" his friend queried. "I have heard you often enough saying you do not believe in fate, karma, or anything but a man's own will and determination."

"I have always believed myself to be my own master," the Prince agreed, looking out the window, "I used to tell myself I had the power to make my life what I wanted it to be. Whatever I might do, I was in control. There was no question of my being manipulated by anyone else, whether human or superhuman."

"And now?" Lord Marston questioned.

"I feel as if I am being swept away on a tidal wave," the Prince said. "I know that I have to meet Lokita, that it was fate that made you take me to the Theatre."

"Nonsense!" Lord Marston said firmly. "You are only feeling like this because the girl has refused to have supper with you. Perhaps she will relent if you ask her often enough. In the meantime, I am not going to cart you about sullen and unco-operative as you were yesterday evening."

"Who is she? How can I find her? Where does she live?" the Prince asked fiercely.

"I dare say, if you set your mind to it you will discover all these things," Lord Marston replied. "In the meantime, as it is only five in the morning, do you mind going to bed and letting me go back to sleep?"

"The trouble with you, Hugo," the Prince said, "is that you cannot raise your eyes to the stars because your feet are so firmly planted on the ground beneath them."

He went out of the room and slammed the door.

Lord Marston laughed and snuggling down in bed shut his eyes.

It was good for Ivan, he told himself, not to get exactly what he wanted the moment he wanted it. He had been too spoilt all his life, and this was a lesson which was long overdue.

As he fell asleep Lord Marston was thinking how envious his friends would be when they saw Suliman.

* * *

Riding in the Bois the following morning with Serge beside her, Lokita found herself thinking of the Prince and feeling sure he was an exceptional rider.

She had often read how magnificently the Russians, like the Hungarians, rode, and about the wildness of their horses and their great endurance.

It was when she was alone with Serge that she could talk of Russia and not feel the constraint which Andy always put on the subject.

Serge, who came from South Russia, had been in her service ever since she could remember. He was her body-guard, her protector, and she knew that her father had trusted him implicitly.

He was a tall, gaunt man with high cheek-bones, and at any time, were it necessary, he would have died for Lokita as he would have done for her father.

But even Serge, Lokita thought as they rode among the trees, had secrets that he would not reveal to her.

They were secrets, she knew, imposed on him by Andy, and because she was sensitive she would not embarrass the Russian by asking him things he had been told not to repeat to her.

But, she thought, it was all so puzzling.

Why must she lead such a strange, lonely life with only three people to whom she could talk without constraint?

With her many instructors and tutors it was different.

She could understand that she must keep them at arm's length and that she must not allow them to encroach on her private life, even though she was aware that many of them were curious.

"You have the brain of a man, *M'mselle*," her elderly teacher of literature had said to her. "What do you intend to do with so much learning?"

"To do with it?" Lokita asked.

"Talents should be used, my dear young lady," he had replied. "Perhaps you should write a book or converse with the great brains that are to be found in Paris at this moment."

He considered a moment before he went on:

"How I would like you to meet some of the celebrated figures in contemporary art and literature like Arsène Houssaye, Dumas, Gustave Flaubert, or even George Sands."

"I would like to meet them too," Lokita said. "You have made so many of their creations live for me by the way you have explained them."

"You should start a Salon of your own, *M'mselle,*" her tutor said, but Lokita shook her head.

That conversation had taken place two months ago, before necessity had obliged her to earn money by dancing.

It was impossible to forget Miss Anderson's face when she had come into the room holding a letter in her hand.

"What is it, Andy?" Lokita had asked.

"A letter from your father's Solicitors."

At the mention of her father's name the tears had come into Lokita's beautiful eyes.

It was only six weeks since they had learnt that he had died in London, and she would never be happy again.

She loved him so deeply, the handsome, brilliant man who was forced by circumstances, which neither he nor anyone else would explain to her, to visit her only occasionally.

It was all something to do with her mother, Lokita knew, and yet what it was or why there had to be so much secrecy she had no idea.

She only knew that to speak of her mother would bring an inexpressible sadness to her father's face, and so, because she loved him, in their precious times together she talked of other things.

She could remember her mother but her image grew more shadowy as the years passed by.

'I was seven when I saw her last,' Lokita thought, 'and that was only for a day.'

Her father's yacht, in which Lokita had enjoyed every moment of the voyage through the Black Sea, had anchored in the Harbour at Odessa late one evening, and when it was dark he had gone ashore.

He had not returned that night, but the following morning he had said:

"Lokita, I am taking you to meet a very great friend of mine. She is a very beautiful lady and a friend of your Mama's."

Lokita had not been particularly interested. It was more exciting to be on the yacht, but her father had taken her ashore to a Villa standing in a magnificent garden, and there under the trees a lady was waiting for them.

Lokita thought many years later that the reason why they had met in the garden was so that nothing they said could be overheard.

She was at the time, however, bewildered because the lady at the sight of her burst into tears. Then going down on her knees and holding her close she had kissed her over and over again.

"My sweet! My darling! My beloved little Lokita!" she had said through her tears.

It was seven years later before Lokita was to realise that the lady who had wept over her was in fact her mother.

Her father had come to see her in Paris in the little house he had bought for her near the Bois, and when he arrived Lokita realised immediately that something had happened.

"What is it, Papa?" she asked.

"I have just received some very sad news," her father answered.

He spoke dully and there was so much pain in his voice that Lokita instinctively put her arms round him.

Always when he came to see her he had been so happy that it seemed to radiate from him and she had found herself laughing with happiness too.

But this was different.

"What is it, Papa?"

"Your mother is—dead!" her father replied with difficulty.

"Dead?" Lokita repeated. "But I did not ... know she was ... alive."

"She has been alive all these years," her father replied, "but it was impossible for her to see you again. We thought it was kinder for you to believe she had died."

"Why was it impossible?" Lokita asked.

"I cannot tell you that," her father replied. "You must trust me, Lokita, as you always have."

"Of course I trust you, Papa, but it is very puzzling. Why did I not know about Mama? And why can I not live with you as other children live with their fathers?"

"One day perhaps I will be able to explain all these things," her father said, "but for the moment it is impossible. You have to believe me, my dearest daughter—it is impossible!"

"What was my mother like?" Lokita asked.

"Do you not remember her when you went to Odessa?"

"Was that my Mama? She was very beautiful."

"The most beautiful person in the world," her father said.

There was a throb in his voice which told Lokita how much he was suffering.

She knew there was no point in asking innumerable questions which he could not answer, so instead she first held him close and kissed him.

Then because she knew it would please him she danced for him.

Madame Albertini had been employed to teach her ball-room dancing on her father's insistence that she should have all the graces and talents of other girls of her age, and it was she who had found that Lokita had an aptitude for mime.

Madame Albertini had trained as a ballet-dancer, but quite early in her career she had slipped on stage and broken her leg, and could no longer continue to dance.

Because she was so expert in ballet she had taken a few pupils among the aristocratic French families and had found that one way of helping them to move gracefully was to teach them to express their feelings by gesture.

Many of the French débutantes who would have been gawky and ungainly acquired a new grace under *Madame*'s tuition, and her fame spread.

In Lokita she had found a pupil so outstandingly responsive, so fantastic in her ability to express what she was thinking, that *Madame* went into eulogies of delight after every lesson.

"It is a crying shame that she has no-one to see her perform," she said over and over again to Miss Anderson.

She could not understand the repressed manner in which her enthusiasm was received.

"The Princess Matilda invites artistes of all sorts to her soirées," *Madame* said. "One of Musset's *proverbes* was acted in her Salon, and *La Revanche de Scapin,* by Théodore de Bauville, was performed to an audience which included the Emperor and Empress."

She looked at Miss Anderson and said persuasively:

"If I were to drop one word to the Princess she would invite Lokita not only as a performer but also as one of her guests."

"No!" Miss Anderson said firmly. "As you well know, *Madame,* when you came here to teach Lokita you promised that you would never mention the child's existence outside the four walls of this house."

"I know! I know!" *Madame* agreed. "But she is so talented! It is a crime that she should hide such a vibrant light under such a very small bushel."

Madame had laughed at her own joke, but Miss Anderson had not joined in.

When the crisis came, when Miss Anderson learnt from the Solicitors that enquiries were being made about the money Lokita had been left by her father, she had turned to *Madame* for help.

"Are you really telling me that this child, who has been brought up in luxury, is now completely penniless?" *Madame* asked.

"I have a little saved," Miss Anderson said. "A very little. We could of course sell this house, but where could we go? As it belongs to Lokita, we pay no rent and it would therefore be cheaper to stay here."

"Far cheaper!" *Madame* agreed firmly. "Rents are soaring in Paris. Baron Haussmann has pulled down half the cheaper houses and erected Civic Halls in their place."

It was a popular grievance and Miss Anderson did not wish to be drawn into an argument over it.

"I was wondering if it would be possible, *Madame*, for Lokita to help you with your pupils and perhaps earn a little money in that way?"

"A waste of time and talent!" *Madame* said. "She should perform on the stage."

"Impossible!" Miss Anderson said. "Absolutely impossible!"

She was still saying the same thing after forty-eight hours of endless arguments; but finally because things were desperate she capitulated.

"But why can I not receive the money which Papa left me?" Lokita asked when it was explained to her.

"Because your father's sister, your aunt, is a nosy, inquisitive woman," Miss Anderson replied. "Your father was always afraid of her finding out that you existed."

"But why should she not do so?" Lokita asked.

She knew the answer before Andy replied:

"There are reasons—very good reasons—why your existence must be kept a secret."

"Now that Papa is dead, will you not tell me what they are?" she asked.

"You will know one day," Miss Anderson promised, "but not yet. It is impossible!"

Lokita had grown to hate that word.

It was "impossible" for her to do this, "impossible" for her to do that, "impossible" to make friends, "impossible" now to discuss Prince Ivan Volkonski, let alone accept his flowers and his present.

But despite the number of times Andy had said "impossible," she had been allowed to earn what seemed to her really enormous sums of money in the Théâtre Impérial Châtelet.

It was, of course, *Madame* Albertini who had brought the Proprietor and the Stage Manager to see her dance.

Lokita had been perceptive enough when the two gentlemen arrived at the tiny house in the Bois to realise they were extremely sceptical of what they would find.

She could almost see the words "amateur" and "impossible" forming on their lips.

In their frock-coats, holding their canes and their high-crowned hats, they had sat down on the sofa in the small Salon and *Madame* had gone to the piano.

"Do not be nervous, *chérie*," she had said in a low voice to Lokita, who was wearing the simple white gown that she wore for her lessons.

She was determined not to be nervous because she knew that this was a test of her ability. She also had the inescapable feeling within herself that her father would not wish her to give anything but her best.

She thought first of *Madame,* who had taken so much trouble not only in persuading the gentlemen to come and see her but also overcoming Miss Anderson's objections.

Then when she began to think of her father it was easy.

She danced for him as she had danced when he visited her, feeling that the music told her what to do, feeling that she expressed not only what was in her mind and her heart but also in her soul.

She danced, forgetting everything but what she was trying to say without words.

Only as she finished and there was a stunned silence did she realise that she had been an unqualified success.

Riding now along the Bois, Lokita had suddenly a strange thought.

In a way it was so revolutionary that she surprised herself.

She thought she would like to dance alone for Prince Ivan and see the appreciation in his dark eyes.

She had known he would be in the audience last night before he came round to the stage-door. She had known that he would be one of the hundreds of other people who had applauded her so wildly, and shouted for her to take a bow, which was one of the things Andy had forbidden and which had been written into her contract.

That was very different from dancing as she danced for her father, feeling his sympathy and understanding reaching out to her.

Then she could tell him of her happiness, her joys, and her anxieties when he had been unable to visit her for a long time.

When she had finished dancing she would run to him and put her arms round his neck and he would hold her very close and kiss her before he spoke.

Lokita felt herself blushing.

"Of course, I would not do that to the Prince!" she told herself. "But still, I would like to dance for him alone."

Chapter Three

Lokita and Serge galloped in an unfashionable part of the Bois where there were few social figures to be seen driving.

It was the Emperor who had decided to turn the Bois de Boulogne into an English Park, and a number of the French thought that he had ruined what before had been a wild Paradise.

Now, as someone had said: "Even the ducks are mechanical and the trees look as if they were painted on a canvas for the Théâtre des Variétés."

But there were still parts of it where neither the Emperor nor Monsieur Varé, his landscape gardener, had encroached, and this was where Lokita rode.

With her cheeks bright with colour after the exercise, she reined in her horse under the shady branches of a tree, and as Serge drew alongside her she said in what was a deliberately casual voice:

"When you were in Russia, Serge, did you ever hear the name Volkonski?"

"But of course, My *Knyīeza*," Serge answered, "it is the name of a noble and famous family."

When they were alone, Serge always called Lokita *Knyīeza*, which meant Princess.

She remembered him often saying to her when she

was very small: "Let me take you for a ride on my shoulders, my little *Knyīeza*," and he would lift her up while she laughed with delight at being so high off the ground.

It annoyed Miss Anderson now that he did not address her as *"Mademoiselle."*

"We are in France, Serge," she would say severely, "and you should speak of *'Mademoiselle'* Lokita."

Serge would bow his head as if obedient to the command, but when he and Lokita were alone he reverted to the name by which she knew he always thought of her.

"Tell me about the Volkonskis," she asked now.

"It is a long time ago since I heard of them, *Knyīeza*," he replied, "but I remember they were very rich, very powerful, and related to the Holy Father."

"To Tsar Nicholas?" Lokita questioned, knowing that Serge was speaking of Nicholas I, who had been the Tsar when he was in Russia.

As she expected, Serge's eyes clouded as they always did when he spoke of Nicholas I, who Lokita knew from her history books had, at the time, been the most alarming Sovereign in Europe.

On his succession to the throne he had lost no time in turning his vast Empire into a barracks. To him, Sovereignty was merely an extension of Army discipline.

Once Lokita, intrigued by what she had read, had asked her father about Tsar Nicholas.

There had been a pause before he answered; then he said in a voice she hardly recognised:

"His ice-cold gaze struck terror into the hearts of his Courtiers and everyone in St. Petersburg."

"Was he cruel, Papa?"

"Unbelievably so," her father replied. "He banished Prince Yussupov to the Caucasus because he was having a love-affair of which his mother did not approve, and one of his most alarming actions was his habit of declaring people insane if he did not agree with them."

"He must have been horrible, Papa!" Lokita exclaimed.

"He was hated by every Russian man, woman, and child," her father answered in a hard voice. "The world is a better place now."

He spoke with such violence that Lokita knew that even to mention Tsar Nicholas affected him personally. So she asked him no more questions but she read all she could find about him.

He had, she learnt, thought nothing of employing thousands of workmen to transform gardens into Oriental Palaces or Ball-Rooms into gardens complete with rockeries and fountains.

The supper-table at the Winter Palace could seat a thousand people, and although the temperature outside was far below freezing-point, the Galleries bloomed with so many exotic flowers that the guests had the illusion of a summer's day.

Yet the poverty and squalor amongst the peasants was unbelievable. Even some of the officials whom he dressed in uniform had their feet tied up with rags.

Men were shipped or sent to Siberia for the most trivial offence, and although the death penalty had been abolished it was clearly understood that a man could be killed by the Knout.

Nicholas was certainly eccentric besides being cruel.

He insisted that Professors, students, engineers, and members of the Civil-Service should all wear uniforms.

Only the Army had the right to wear moustaches, and all moustaches had to be black, dyed if necessary.

The Tsar with his Secret Police instigated a régime of terror.

And yet, Lokita read, he was one of the most handsome men in the whole country.

The history books were often cold and dry, and she liked to hear about Russia from Serge, even though he could tell her very little of what she wished to know.

She thought over what he had said now about Prince Ivan Volkonski, and almost as if she conjured him up out of her imagination she saw him riding towards her over the same open ground on which she and Serge had just galloped.

She recognised him immediately.

No-one else, she thought, wore his hat at exactly that angle on his head; no-one else could look so magnificent on the black stallion, which was as outstanding as his rider.

The Prince drew nearer, and now she could see those strange, dark eyes that she had peeped at from the shadows in the Theatre and curve of his lips that made him look as if he were faintly mocking.

Lokita realised that both the Prince and his companion were excellent riders.

But there was something in the way the Prince sat a horse which gave her the impression of exhilaration, of a wildness that was very Slavic.

Now she could hear the thunder of the horses' hoofs and they passed her so swiftly that it was as if a typhoon had swept over her.

Then she could only stare at the Prince's back as he and the man beside him galloped on and were finally lost to sight among the trees.

"That was Prince Ivan Volkonski," she said in a low voice.

"He rides like a Russian," Serge remarked, and it was a compliment.

They rode back to the little house where Miss Anderson was waiting for them, but Lokita did not relate whom they had seen during their ride.

After a light meal Miss Anderson insisted on Lokita resting because she had a performance to give that evening. She lay in her small bed-room, not sleeping but thinking of the Prince.

She liked his name.

"Ivan Volkonski," she murmured to herself, and thought by comparison how dull her own name sounded.

Lokita Lawrence.

There was nothing very romantic about it, but she knew, although no-one had ever told her so, that Lawrence was not her real name, nor that of her father.

It had been obvious, ever since she was old enough to think, that the name did not come easily to Andy's lips: when she addressed her father by the name of Lawrence there was always a little pause as if she forced herself to substitute one name for another.

'But what is the use of asking questions?' Lokita thought.

She never received answers to them and the mystery of who she was and where she came from seemed only to deepen as the years went by.

Now it was worse than it had ever been before.

Who was this aunt whose enquiries had prevented her from taking the money which her father had left her?

"I have made you safe for life, my darling," he had said to her once. "Things may be difficult for you, but you will always have all you need."

Because she loved him Lokita had not said that what she wanted more than anything else was to live with him, have friends like other girls, and eventually marry someone she loved.

Because it would have pained him to hear her speak in such a manner, she bit back the words which had come to her lips and instead reassured him that she was happy, which indeed in many ways she was.

She wanted to learn, and she found that the instruction given on all the many subjects which filled her days was interesting; and what tutors did not teach her she learnt for herself from books.

She and Andy would visit the Museums and the Theatres, usually having seats at a matinée because Miss Anderson did not like going out at night.

They would explore the outskirts of Paris and they would attend Services at various Churches, including Notre Dame.

"What religion am I?" Lokita had asked once, and Andy had hesitated before she answered:

"Your father is Church of England."

"And my mother?"

Again there was a pause before almost reluctantly Andy said:

"She was Russian Orthodox."

"That is why the only thing I have of hers is the ikon in my bed-room."

She had had it ever since childhood, and it was a beautiful ikon, very old, set in a frame of diamonds, amethysts, and pearls.

Sometimes Lokita would touch it as if she thought it could tell her about her mother.

It was hard to remember the lady who had held her in her arms and cried.

Of one thing Lokita was absolutely sure: everything which was Russian appealed to her.

She was well aware also that it was the Russian part of her blood of which Miss Anderson was afraid.

"Tell me about Mama," she would plead.

But Andy would shake her head and talk about her father and how kind and honourable he was.

That also was cold comfort when she saw so little of him.

Now for the first time, Lokita told herself, she was like a butterfly emerging from its chrysalis.

She could hardly believe it possible that in the last month she had actually been allowed to dance on the stage.

Granted, even there she was made to behave in an extraordinary manner, speaking to no-one in the Theatre, taken to the wings by Andy, and hurried away as soon as she had changed her clothes.

Yet it was like coming out of prison, a prison that had been a very pleasant one, and yet the doors and windows had been barred.

Lying on her bed with her eyes shut, Lokita wondered what would have happened if she had gone out to supper with the Prince as he had invited her to do.

She had read and reread the sentence he had written on the back of the card:

Have supper with me and you will make me the happiest man in the world!

Of course, she told herself, it was only a conventional phrase, and yet she had the feeling that she would have liked to make him happy.

There was something about him she could not explain that had appealed to her, as his flowers had done. Even the butterfly brooch which Andy considered an insult had been in exquisite taste.

"I suppose I shall never talk to him," she told herself with a little sigh.

But something inside her rebelled fiercely at the thought.

As usual, they drove to the Theatre in the hired *fiacre* which Serge fetched for them when it was time to leave their little house.

Lokita thought Miss Anderson would have liked to take Serge with them as a body-guard, but considered it might cause unnecessary comment and seem ostentatious.

This was another reason why she did not hire a carriage to take them to the Theatre and wait to take them back again.

The other performers took *fiacres* from the rank outside the Theatre and only the ladies who had wealthy protectors had their own carriages or were collected by the gentlemen who wished to show them off at one of the many fashionable places for supper.

Tonight as Lokita waited in the wings, instead of concentrating on her dance and what she intended to express she peeped through the curtains at the audience.

The Theatre was packed as usual and there had

been a big round of applause for the Azure Lake and the nymphs swimming in it.

As she looked at the long rows of people sitting in the stalls, the women glittering with jewellery, the men with their stiff white shirts, Lokita was conscious almost for the first time that her audience consisted of people—real people—flesh and blood that moved, thought, and felt as she did herself.

Before, because she had thought only of her dance while the footlights made everything beyond them seem nothing but a blue haze, the audience had been only a noise without substance.

She raised her eyes from the stalls to the boxes and now she saw him on the other side of the Theatre in the big box with its red velvet curtains and gold ornamentation.

He was alone, there was nobody with him, and he was not looking at the stage on which the comedians were performing but glancing round the auditorium, his fingers tapping the edge of the box as if he was impatient.

"Lokita!"

Miss Anderson's voice was sharp and Lokita let the curtain through which she had been peeping fall back into place.

"Concentrate and think only of your dance," Andy said in a tone which made Lokita feel guilty.

She drew in her breath slowly and rhythmically as *Madame* Albertini had taught her to do. Then the comedians were bouncing off the stage to waves of applause, and the lights were going down.

Lokita knew then that tonight she would dance for the Prince as she had danced for her father.

As usual the music swept her away so that she felt rather than thought what she portrayed.

Within her, almost like a secret she held in her breast, was the knowledge that everything she did, every movement she made, was for the man who was watching her.

It was almost as if they were alone and no-one else was there.

Because of her desire to please him, every movement seemed even more real, more compelling than it had ever been before.

When she left the stage after her second dance, the other performers standing in the wings, and even the stage-hands, were applauding her.

"Magnifique!" "Bravo!" "Vous êtes superbe!"

Their complimentary exclamations followed her as Andy hurried her up the iron stairs to the dressing-room.

"Hurry, hurry!" she was saying.

Pushing the flowers to one side, she came behind the curtain to help Lokita out of her Grecian robe and into her ordinary clothes.

She was obviously in such a fever to leave the Theatre that Lokita knew quite well that she too was aware that Prince Ivan had been in the Royal Box.

As she fastened the last button at the back of Lokita's gown, Miss Anderson put her cloak over her shoulders and had the door of the dressing-room open before Lokita had pulled the hood over her head.

They hurried down the iron staircase and Lokita thought that Andy gave a sigh of relief that there was no-one waiting for them at the stage-door.

They got into the nearest *fiacre* and the *cocher* whipped up his horses.

As usual, the carriage smelt of decaying leather, hay, and dirt.

Lokita lay back not exhausted but feeling depleted, as if she had given out so much of herself that she was almost empty inside.

'Had he received what she was trying to give him?' she wondered, and because her feelings had been so intense she was glad that Andy did not wish to speak to her.

They had passed along the Boulevards and were

now in quieter, more residential streets which led towards the Bois.

Suddenly there was the sound of men's voices and the *cocher* drew his horses to a standstill.

Even as Miss Anderson bent forward to ask: "What is happening?" the door was flung open and a man climbed into the carriage.

He wore a black mask and carried a pistol in his hand.

Lokita gave a little cry and Miss Anderson, putting an arm round her protectively, asked angrily:

"Who are you and what do you want?"

"There is nothing to be frightened of, *Mesdames,*" the man said. "You will not be hurt if you come with me quietly."

"Come where?" Miss Anderson asked.

"That you will learn later."

"This is an outrage! You have no right to behave in such a manner!

"There is nothing you can do about it," the man said, "so sit quiet."

He spoke with an accent that proclaimed he was not an educated person but a servant.

A superior servant, Lokita thought, but in that class.

There was still the sound of voices outside and she had the idea that another man had climbed onto the box and taken the reins from the *cocher*.

Certainly the horses were moving quicker.

While she knew that Andy was seething with anger and was at the same time apprehensive, she herself was not really afraid.

It had been a shock to see the man with the mask climb into the carriage, but it was so like a burlesque or part of the pantomime that it did not seem real.

If they were being kidnapped, if that was what was happening, what could be the reason for it? They certainly had very little money with which to pay ransom.

Then Lokita thought that because she had an important role at the Theatre perhaps this man and his accomplices thought they could extort a large sum from the Producers of *Cinderella,* who would not wish to lose her act.

She was well aware that the newspapers had acclaimed her as the one artiste who was original and unusual in the whole production.

Théophile Gautier, the author and poet, who had reviewed *Cinderella* in *Le Rire,* had done so with admiration and weariness, but about her he had been unprecedentedly enthusiastic.

"That must be the reason for this hold-up," Lokita told herself.

She hoped that the little "nest-egg" of her earnings which Andy had deposited in the Bank every Friday would not be swept away when they needed it so badly.

They drove on in silence, the masked man continually glancing out the window as if he was in a hurry to arrive.

Then the gas-lights seemed to increase and the road was wider and more impressive and Lokita had the idea, although she was not sure, that they were near the Champs Élysées.

They drove on past some iron railings and came to a standstill outside the portico of what appeared to be a large house.

The man sitting with them opened the door and stepped out.

"Will you please alight, *Mesdames?*" he said.

"I wish to know where you have brought us and what this place is," Miss Anderson demanded.

"Everything will be explained later," the masked man replied. "Kindly alight without further argument."

It was obvious that they must obey him, and Miss Anderson stepped out first, followed by Lokita.

She saw that there were two other men besides the

one who had sat with them inside the carriage and she thought it must have been a considerable crush on the box and was sorry for the *cocher*.

But there was no time to consider anything.

The door of the house was opened and they were hurried inside.

There were a few candles standing, strangely enough, on the floor, and Lokita soon realised that the house was empty and unfurnished, and they were walking along a passage thick with dust.

A door was opened and they were ushered into what must have once been a Salon. It too was empty, with the exception of two hard chairs.

On the mantelpiece there were three candles which made the shadows in the large room seem dark and eerie.

"Will you kindly tell us why we have been brought here?" Miss Anderson asked, and her voice seemed to ring round the empty Salon.

"When my master arrives he will explain everything to you," the masked man replied.

He had walked ahead of them, still holding his pistol in his right hand. He indicated the chairs.

"Be seated, *Mesdames*," he said. "You will not be bound if you do not attempt to escape, and you will not be gagged if you do not scream."

Proudly, as if she were walking to the guillotine, Miss Anderson swept towards one of the chairs and sat down on it.

Lokita, who had followed her, occupied the other.

The man shut the door and leant against the wall, watching them.

"You must not be frightened," Miss Anderson said to Lokita in English. "I do not think they mean to hurt us, but I am afraid we may have to pay for our release."

"I have been thinking that too," Lokita replied. "How much do you think they will ask?"

"They cannot have more than we have in the Bank," Miss Anderson replied.

Her lips tightened and Lokita knew how much it would hurt her to give away the money they had accumulated after so much argument.

Andy had fought so fiercely against her going on the stage, and only when she was convinced that there was nothing else they could do did she capitulate to *Madame* Albertini's insistence.

Now the money was all to be swept away by these robbers—these bandits.

"I imagine," Miss Anderson said, speaking in a different tone, "that the real owner of this house would be somewhat surprised if he knew to what use it was being put."

"It must be someone important," Lokita said, "it is very large and impressive."

"I only hope the Police will apprehend these villains and they are transported."

Lokita was about to reply when suddenly there was a tremendous commotion outside the room.

Men were shouting and it sounded as if a pitched battle was taking place. Two pistol-shots rang out!

It was so intimidating that almost before they realised what they were doing Miss Anderson and Lokita had risen to their feet to hold on to each other.

The man in the room who had been watching them exclaimed:

"*Sacré nom!* We must have been betrayed!"

He pulled open the door and joined in the melee outside.

"What can be happening?" Lokita asked in a whisper.

"Perhaps we can escape," Miss Anderson suggested.

Even as she turned towards the window the door opened again and a man came into the room. As Lokita looked at him her heart leapt and turned over.

It was the Prince!

He had a pistol in his right hand.

As he advanced towards them he transferred it to his left hand and said in English:

"It is all right, ladies. You are safe! I am Prince Ivan Volkonski, and my servants are dealing with the *canaille* who abducted you."

"Who are they? What did they want?" Lokita asked.

Her eyes were shining as she looked up at him, and she wanted to put out her hands towards him because she was so glad that he had rescued them.

"They are the scum of the back-streets," he answered. "This is not the first time they have kidnapped a celebrity for ransom."

"That is what I suspected was happening," Miss Anderson said in a calm voice.

"As I do not wish you to see anything unpleasant," the Prince said, "may I suggest that we leave this house in a somewhat unconventional manner?"

He opened one of the large casements as he spoke. Then with a smile on his lips he said to Miss Anderson:

"Shall I go first, *Madame,* and assist you to the ground?"

"I should imagine that would be best," Miss Anderson replied.

She spoke in such a severe tone that Lokita felt she was being somewhat ungrateful considering that the Prince had come to their rescue.

He stepped over the window-sill and assisted first Miss Anderson to the ground, then Lokita.

She felt his arms go round her as he lifted her.

It gave her a rather strange sensation, but of course she was not aware that his heart was thundering in his breast and the pulses were throbbing in his temples.

He set her down gently, then taking her by the hand he said:

"The garden of my house adjoins this. There is a door just ahead of us."

His fingers felt very strong and warm.

Because it was dark Lokita was glad that he was helping her over the grass, for it was difficult to see where she was going.

But the Prince seemed to know his way and she fancied that on his other side he put his hand under Miss Anderson's elbow.

Vaguely she wondered what had happened to his pistol and thought he must have thrown it down when he helped them from the window.

'He may need it again,' she thought apprehensively, and looked back just in case the masked men were following them.

"You need not be afraid," the Prince said as if he sensed what she was thinking. "My servants will take those who are still alive and hand them over to the Police. The authorities deal very effectively with such malefactors, I can assure you."

"Those who are alive . . . !" Lokita repeated beneath her breath, and thought how heroic it was of him to have fought and killed to save her.

They reached the gate in the wall and the Prince pushed it open.

Then they were in a large garden filled with flowers and lit by lanterns hanging from branches of many of the trees.

It was so pretty that it might have been one of the scenes from *Cinderella* and Lokita looked at it with delight until she was aware that the Prince's eyes were on her face.

"We are extremely grateful to you," Miss Anderson said sharply, as if she wished to draw attention to her presence, "but now we would ask Your Highness to call us another *fiacre* so that we can return home."

"There are reasons why you should not be in too much of a hurry," the Prince said quietly.

"What reasons?" Miss Anderson queried.

"The three men who kidnapped you will not be the instigators of this crime," he said. "Whoever instructed them was, I think, to have arrived later to inform you of the ransom that was expected and to ask you to sign a cheque for it."

Lokita drew in her breath.

"And if we had . . . refused?"

"They would have kept you there until you paid," the Prince replied. "As it is, I suspect you would have had to wait in that empty room until the Banks opened and the cheque could be cashed."

As he spoke they were walking towards the house, and now he led the way up some broad white marble steps and onto a terrace where there were long French windows glowing with a golden light.

One of them was open and they entered a *Salon* that was so enormous and so beautiful that Lokita gave an involuntary exclamation of delight.

There were hundreds of candles burning in crystal chandeliers and their soft light revealed far more effectively than gas-lamps would have done the superlative furniture, the fine pictures, and the profusion of *objets d'art* that covered every side-table.

"May I welcome you to my house?" the Prince said. "And I can only regret, ladies, that you had to suffer so much discomfort before you could become my guests."

"Your Highness's house is magnificent!" Lokita said in a low voice.

The Prince did not answer, but he was looking at her in a manner which made her feel shy.

A servant appeared at the door and the Prince gave him an order in Russian.

"Will you sit down?" he asked courteously, reverting to English.

Miss Anderson seated herself in an arm-chair, holding herself stiffly with a straight back as if she was impatient to be gone.

Lokita undid her velvet cloak at the neck and the Prince took it from her and laid it on a chair at the side of the room.

"May I look at some of your beautiful things?" she begged with the eagerness of a child.

"I should be honoured," he replied.

She moved to a table covered with snuff-boxes that she knew were not only of great value but of historic interest.

Some of them were set with miniatures of Catherine the Great and surrounded by diamonds; others portrayed the Tsars and handsome men who she thought must be the Prince's ancestors.

The enamel work, the settings of the precious stones, and the engravings were finer than anything she had seen before even in Museums.

She touched them delicately with one finger, feeling she must remember them when they were no longer in front of her eyes.

The servants brought in a round table which they covered with a cloth of Venetian lace, then laid three places for supper.

There was gold plate engraved with the Prince's coat-of-arms, there were crystal glasses edged with gold, and there was a wine-cooler, also of gold, that held half a dozen bottles of wine.

The Prince invited his guests to the table as the servants presented them with caviar set in a great block of blue-white ice.

Miss Anderson was offered vodka, which she refused, and so did Lokita.

"You must have a little champagne," the Prince said. "I feel, ladies, you both need it after the shock you have experienced."

Miss Anderson seemed about to refuse; then, as if the golden wine in the engraved glass persuaded her almost against her will, she raised it to her lips.

"I do not think I really like champagne," Lokita said.

She had drunk it once or twice with her father and found it disappointing after all she had read about it being the "wine of happiness" and the "nectar of the gods."

The Prince smiled.

"When you have passed through a great many different emotions in your life," he said, "you will find that champagne is the only wine with which you can express delight or sweep away sorrow. Tonight I drink with delight and gratitude because two such charming ladies are my guests."

The last word was in the plural but he looked at Lokita.

As the servants brought in many exotic and delicious dishes, which were, surprisingly, ready, although Lokita imagined that the Prince had ordered them earlier for himself, their host set himself out to be agreeable.

He talked to Miss Anderson, exerting the irresistible charm for which he was famous, and with a perception which was almost clairvoyant he found the subjects which interested her.

He asked no awkward questions, he merely talked as if he were in a Salon surrounded by the greatest intellects of Paris.

No woman, whatever her age or however prejudiced she might be against him, could have resisted such an insidious compliment.

As the meal drew to a close Miss Anderson was laughing and responding to the Prince in a manner which made Lokita stare at her wide-eyed.

Never had she known Andy to be so animated or in fact look so young. The years seemed to have slipped away and the lines of worry had vanished from her face.

"Will you have French or Turkish coffee?" the Prince asked as the dessert was taken from the table.

"I think Turkish coffee would be a treat," Miss Anderson replied.

"And you, *Mademoiselle?*" the Prince asked Lokita.

"I have always longed to taste real Turkish coffee," she answered.

The Prince gave an order and the servants brought in the coffee and set it on a side-table just inside the door. Then they removed the table on which they had dined.

Miss Anderson moved into the more comfortable arm-chair which she had occupied before supper.

"I will bring you your coffee," the Prince said with his back to them, "and also a small liqueur."

"No, no!" Miss Anderson protested. "I must not have any more, and it is time, Your Highness, that we left."

"Only when you have finished your meal," the Prince answered, "and what meal in Paris would be complete without coffee and liqueur at the end of it?"

He carried in one hand a handleless cup set in a holder of gold ornamented with emeralds, and in the other, a glass containing a liqueur, which he set down on the small table at Miss Anderson's side.

Then he brought Lokita her coffee but he did not persuade her to have a liqueur.

"Surely these coffee cups are unique?" she said, raising the gold and emerald holder in her hand.

"They were given to me by the Sultan of Turkey," the Prince explained, "and it was when I was staying in Constantinople that I learnt exactly how Turkish coffee should be made."

"It is certainly delicious," Miss Anderson said.

She drank a little, sipped her liqueur, then drank a little more coffee.

Lokita took a few small sips and decided she would not be in a hurry to finish her cup, for she was sure that when she had done so Andy would insist on returning home, and she had no wish to go.

It had been an excitement she could not explain to herself to have supper with the Prince, even though he had talked all the time to Andy and indeed had hardly looked at her.

In an effort to prolong their visit Lokita asked:

"Do you think I could look again at your treasures?"

"Of course," the Prince replied.

He rose to his feet and glanced at Miss Anderson as if expecting her to protest once again that they must leave.

She was however sitting back comfortably in the arm-chair, a smile on her lips.

She said nothing as Lokita passed her to go towards the table arranged with the valuable snuff-boxes she had been examining before supper.

As she looked down at them the Prince was beside her and because he was so near she felt a little quiver go through her.

"You have so many beautiful things," she said, feeling she must say something.

"But nothing as beautiful as you!"

She was so surprised that she turned up her face to look at him. She found that her eyes were so held by his that it was hard to look away.

"Come and sit down," the Prince said. "I want to talk to you."

Lokita looked over her shoulder at Miss Anderson and saw to her astonishment that her head was lying back against the cushions of the chair and she was asleep.

The Prince followed her glance.

"It often happens," he said. "When someone has been through a time of mental or physical stress, they fall asleep."

As he spoke, he took Lokita by the hand and drew her to another sofa by the window opening onto the garden.

She sat down and he seated himself beside her, turning sideways so that he was looking at her.

"You are lovely!" he said in his deep voice. "Incredibly, unbelievably lovely!"

Lokita blushed. Then she said:

"I would like to . . . thank Your Highness for the basket of orchids you sent me."

"But you left them in your dressing-room."

"Miss Anderson . . . thought that your present was an . . . insult. I know you did not mean it . . . like that . . . but it made her . . . angry."

"She was right! It was an insult!" the Prince declared.

Lokita looked at him in astonishment and he went on:

"It was an insult to think I could ornament you with anything so commonplace as diamonds when what I wanted was to take the stars from the sky to make you a necklace and give you the moon to hold in your arms."

There was a depth of emotion in his voice which seemed to vibrate within Lokita.

"Only the rays of the sun could make a wreath for your hair that is worthy," he went on, and there was a passionate note in his voice as he exclaimed: "Lokita! What have you done to me?"

Now it was not only impossible to look away from him but impossible to breathe.

"When I saw you dance," the Prince said, "you spoke to my soul and I knew I had been looking for you all my life. I want you, Lokita, I want you as I have never wanted anything before—but I am afraid!"

"Afraid?"

"You are like a flower," he said; "if I touch you, will you wither and fade?"

Lokita drew in her breath but she could not speak and now very gently the Prince took one of her hands from where it lay in her lap and held it in his.

He looked down at it, at the long, thin fingers that could be so expressive when she danced, the small, soft pink palm with the lines of fate etched on it.

Then he raised it to his mouth.

He did not kiss it, but just barely touched her skin

with his lips, moving them up each of her fingers, then round the outside of the palm and down to her wrist.

He felt her quiver and he asked:

"Does that make you feel?"

"Yes," she whispered slowly.

"What do you feel—tell me."

"It is . . . very strange . . . it is almost like when I am dancing and I feel . . . there are angels and someone whom I love near me . . . but they are outside me . . . what I feel now is . . . inside . . . inside my heart."

"Oh, my darling! My sweet! My *Drouska!* That is what I want you to feel!"

"But . . . why?"

"Because it is what I feel for you. Do you not realise, heart of my heart, soul of my soul, that this is love?"

As he spoke, the Prince passed his lips passionately into the palm of her hand.

Lokita felt as if a streak of lightning ran through her body, passing through her breast and rising in her throat until it reached her lips.

The Prince raised his head.

"I said you were like a flower," he said, "and you are my flower—mine—and no-one shall ever take you from me."

"Andy!" Lokita whispered.

The Prince glanced over his shoulder.

"Leave everything to me," he said. "Like everyone else, she will think it too soon, that we do not know our minds. But you know as I do that this is fate, that we have known each other not only for a few hours, but all through eternity."

"Do you . . . really believe . . . that?"

"I swear it to be true," the Prince said positively, "and if I could I would sweep you up in my arms and carry you away to somewhere where no-one could find us, where we could be alone and where I could teach you, my *Drouska,* about love—the love which burns in me like a flaming fire."

"Can . . . love . . . happen so . . . quickly?" Lokita asked.

"It is not quickly, my star from the sky," he replied. "It is a love which has been there for centuries in perhaps a million lives before this one."

His fingers tightened on hers and he went on:

"In claiming you I am merely reclaiming what is already mine."

"You really . . . believe that?"

"I believe it as I believe in God above," the Prince said. "I believe it as I believe in life itself!"

He kissed her hand again, then he put it in her lap and said:

"You know I want to hold you in my arms, you know I want to kiss your lips, as I know no other man has ever done. But because I love you to distraction, because I know that we shall be together until the stars fall from the skies and the seas run dry, I must give you time, my beautiful darling, time to think."

"I have . . . thought about . . . you ever since I first saw . . . you," Lokita murmured.

She saw the question in his eyes and explained:

"When you came to the Theatre you walked past . . . us as you went up to my . . . dressing-room."

"If only I had known."

"It was better that you did not know. Andy was very angry . . . and she might have been . . . rude to . . . you."

"And you were not angry?"

"I thought you were . . . different from any man I had ever . . . seen before," Lokita said simply.

"As I know you are very different," the Prince said. "Oh, my precious, life of my life, my little flower, I want to kneel at your feet and kiss them because everything about you is so infinitely precious, so perfect, so indescribably beautiful."

"When you . . . talk to me like . . . that," Lokita whispered, "it is like listening to . . . music."

"There is so much I want to give you," the Prince said, "and so much, my perfect little love, that you can give me."

He was about to say more when a sound came from Miss Anderson's lips and they both knew that she yawned and opened her eyes.

Before she could turn her head, the Prince had risen to his feet and walked towards her.

"I think now," he said in the conventional, charming voice he had used during supper, "it will be safe for you to return home."

"Then we must go at once," Miss Anderson said.

She appeared not to realise that she had been asleep, but her eyes blinked for a moment as if they felt heavy. She smoothed down her gown with busy fingers.

"To make quite sure you are safe," the Prince said, "I am taking you home myself."

"There is no need, Your Highness," Miss Anderson replied, but her voice was not peremptory, it was in fact but a formal protest.

"I think there is every need," the Prince answered, "and never again must you both be subjected to the dangers you encountered tonight."

As he spoke he lifted Lokita's velvet cape from the chair on which he had put it.

As he helped her into it she felt his hands against her shoulders and she quivered.

She also thought, although she was not sure, that he kissed her hair.

Then she was following Andy from the Salon into an enormous marble hall in which there were a dozen footmen in a livery ornamented with gold braid.

One of the flunkeys handed the Prince his hat, another handed him his driving-gloves, then they walked out through an impressive door and down the marble steps.

Waiting in the drive outside the house were two carriages.

One was closed and drawn by two horses; the other was an open chaise drawn by four.

The Prince looked at Lokita with a smile.

"Which shall it be?" he asked.

"I have never driven behind four horses," she answered.

"Then this will be a new experience," he answered.

She knew by the look he gave her that he meant it was another experience to add to the one she had already had tonight.

There was room for three of them in the chaise and to protect them from the night air the servants put a rug of white ermine over their knees.

Then, driving superbly with an expertise that Lokita recognised as being exceptional, the Prince drove along the Champs Élysées.

He drove very fast, the horses moving, Lokita thought, like the wind, and she felt she was being carried across the sky by Apollo himself.

Indeed, she was sure that the Prince was enveloped with the same mystical, heavenly light as Apollo.

She knew he had brought a strange and wonderful light into her life and if she ever lost him there would only be an unutterable darkness.

Chapter Four

As Lord Marston stepped out of the carriage he yawned with relief that the evening was over.

He always disliked the more intimate parties which he had to attend at the Tuileries.

The old Palace of Catherine de Médicis had for three hundred years housed a succession of French Sovereigns.

When the Second Empire came into being, the Emperor had to create a Court.

He restored the pomp and ceremony of his uncle's Empire, and, as it was a vital and brilliant age, his Court, which was to be the last, was the most resplendent ever known.

But in spite of all the pomp and circumstance, the food and wine which were served at the Emperor's table were second-rate and, as one guest wrote afterwards:

The food was simple, plentiful, and much like the slightly dated cooking of a conscientious hotel.

After the superlative Chefs employed by the Prince and the outstanding cuisine at the British Embassy,

Lord Marston had found the food as unappetising as the conversation.

The décor had been theatrical and impressive, the ladies in full evening-dress glittering with jewels, the gentlemen in tail-coats and decorations, but what was more sensational was the exotic figure of Scander, the Empress Eugénie's Nubian attendant.

In his gold embroidered robes he looked as if he had stepped out of some eighteenth-century painting.

With such a background it should have been easy to make the conversation interesting, Lord Marston thought. But the Empress made no effort, and although the Emperor attempted to talk there was little to say.

Politics and all delicate subjects were forbidden in front of the servants, and art and literature, except in the Salon of Princess Mathilde, were not socially acceptable and anyway nobody knew very much about them.

When dinner was over the evening seemed to drag on in the Salon, which was unpleasantly hot from the candles of four chandeliers and a fire.

It was to Lord Marston an inexpressible relief when finally he saw that the Emperor and Empress were retiring and he could leave.

Now as he walked into the hall the Prince's Major Domo said:

"His Highness is in the Salon, M'Lord."

Lord Marston, handing his hat and cloak to a servant, walked through the door held open for him by another flunkey.

He was surprised that the Prince was at home, for he thought he had intended to spend the evening with one of the many ladies whose invitations on colourful, scented writing-paper flooded into the house almost every hour of the day.

As he entered the Salon, Lord Marston found his friend standing at the open window, looking out at the garden.

"I am surprised to find you here, Ivan," he said aloud.

The Prince turned round and Lord Marston saw by the blazing look in his eyes and the expression on his face that something untoward had occurred.

"I have seen her! I have talked to her! I have kissed her hand!" -

The words seemed to flow from the Prince's lips like a triumphant oratorio.

Lord Marston moved across the Salon towards him.

"I presume you are speaking of Lokita," he said. "But how is it possible?"

"She is beautiful, Hugo, more beautiful close to than she could ever look on the stage, and she is mine —mine as she was meant to be since the beginning of time!"

His voice seemed to ring out so rapturously that Lord Marston almost expected the crystal drops on the chandeliers to tinkle an accompaniment.

"Suppose you tell me all about it?" he said with a smile, sitting down on the sofa and taking a cigar from a gold box set with huge amethysts from the Siberian mines.

The Prince did not speak and Lord Marston went on:

"It seems incredible that she should have agreed to meet you when everyone else has been refused."

"She did not exactly—agree, not at first," the Prince said, a smile on his lips.

"I have a feeling you have been doing something extraordinarily reprehensible," Lord Marston said. "You had better tell me about it, Ivan."

"You frightened me so much with your stories of the Dragon who guards her, the very English Miss Anderson," the Prince said, "that I knew there was only one way to storm the fortress, and that was by indirect attack."

"I do not like the sound of this," Lord Marston remarked.

"It was not difficult to abduct the two ladies," the Prince went on. "My three secretaries played their parts as bandits most convincingly.

Lord Marston put his hand up to his forehead.

"Ivan! Ivan!" he groaned. "If the newspapers should learn of this!"

"No-one will learn of it," the Prince replied. "They were taken on my instructions to the Château of the *Duc* de Guise next door. It has been empty for over a year."

"And what happened then?"

"I rescued them! The hero in true swashbuckling form!"

"And they were exceedingly grateful to you, I suppose?" Lord Marston asked sarcastically.

"Naturally!" the Prince replied. "But, Hugo, as I lifted her through the window I touched her, and I knew then that what I felt for her was different from what I have ever felt for any woman before."

Lord Marston did not answer, but he looked sceptical. The Prince glanced at him, then walked across the floor restlessly.

"I know that sounds banal and I know exactly what you are thinking. But this *is* different. I worship her, I adore her! She is pure, Hugo, so pure that I did not even attempt to kiss her lips."

"That is certainly unlike your usual buccaneering tactics!" Lord Marston remarked ironically. "As you have so often said to me: 'A man should always take what he wants and argue afterwards.' "

"There was no question of argument," the Prince said, "but I would not take what she is not willing to give."

"You are betting on your irresistible charm that you will not have to wait for long," Lord Marston remarked.

He looked at the Prince, then he said:

"What was the Dragon, as you call her, doing all this time? Did she just sit and watch you kissing the hand and making love to this girl she has guarded so fiercely?"

"She was asleep," the Prince replied.

Lord Marston sat upright.

"Ivan, you have not told me the whole truth: What other crimes have you been perpetrating?"

"Nothing in the least harmful," the Prince replied. "Just a little pill in the coffee, so mild that she did not even realise she had taken it."

"I give up!" Lord Marston cried. "You are impossible! If you think you have won Kingfisher by such behaviour, you are very mistaken."

"I do not want your damned horse!" the Prince answered fiercely. "I do not wish to speak of a wager in the same breath that I speak of Lokita. She is something apart; someone whose name should never be bandied about like that of other women in this loose and profligate city."

Lord Marston looked at him, then said in a surprised voice:

"When you talk like that, Ivan, I begin to believe you really are in love."

"I am in love," the Prince said in a low voice, "but it is much more than that. She is a part of me, an indivisible part. At the same time, I am at her feet, worshipping her, because she is so different from any other woman I have ever met or even imagined."

"And you know all this on so short an acquaintance?" Lord Marston asked.

"I might have known you would not understand," the Prince retorted furiously. "And why should you be expected to do so? You are not a Slav!"

That was true enough, Lord Marston thought, and he knew that the extravagant Slavic temperament was a national attribute, almost a matter of pride like sex to the French.

To all of them, *Dousha*—the soul—was as real and as much a part of their lives as pride and integrity were to an Englishman.

The Prince when he loved would love not only with his heart but with his soul, and if, as it appeared, Lokita had become enshrined in his soul, then Lord Marston knew this was something which had never happened to him before.

The Prince walked to the window and flung back his handsome head to look up at the stars overhead.

"Lokita is a star," he said. "Yet I shall hold her in my arms and she will become mine as she was meant to be when the first star shone in the sky."

* * *

Lord Marston came down to breakfast the following morning to find his host already at the table.

Both men were dressed in riding-clothes, for the Prince invariably rode in the Bois immediately after breakfast and Lord Marston was only too willing to join him, especially as he could ride one of the Prince's superlative horses.

As he entered the room Lord Marston was aware that there was an alertness and a light in the Prince's expressive eyes which warned him that something unusual was about to occur.

"If you have an assignation to meet Lokita," he said as he seated himself at the table, "then there is no reason for me to accompany you."

"I have no assignation," the Prince replied, "but I know where we will find her."

He laughed softly.

"I was very subtle and very diplomatic, Hugo. You would have been proud of me."

"When you did what?" Lord Marston enquired.

"When I extracted from Lokita the information that she rides every morning in the Bois. It was so easy. She admired my horses, I asked her if she rode, and she said it was an exercise which she enjoyed more than anything else except dancing.

"We agreed it was most pleasant in the early morning before the Bois becomes crowded with all the fashion of Paris."

"And her *Duenna* was listening?" Lord Marston asked.

"I had learnt what I wanted to learn," the Prince said, "and I think, if the truth be known, that the Dragon was still a little sleepy."

"I suppose it is no use my telling you that I am appalled by your behaviour," Lord Marston remarked.

"Only Englishmen could quote the proverb 'All is fair in love and war' and then not expect to live up to it!" the Prince retorted.

"Gentlemen are expected to be sportsmen," Lord Marston said severely, "but the way you behaved, Ivan, was like shooting a sitting duck! It was as easy as that!"

"Certainly not," the Prince said. "To boast would be unlucky!"

"Superstitious as well!" Lord Marston teased. "You are certainly involving all the emotions where Lokita is concerned. Let us hope you will not be disappointed."

"I shall never be that," the Prince replied. "Never —do you hear, Hugo?"

"It is difficult not to, considering that you are shouting," Lord Marston answered.

He was hardly allowed to finish his breakfast before the Prince was insisting that they should leave for the Bois.

As they rode up the Champs Élysées it was not surprising that the passers-by turned to look at them, or that women, fascinated by the Prince, watched him until he was out of sight.

When they reached the Bois they trotted through the trees, then galloped in the open space where the Prince rode every morning.

It was over an hour before Lokita appeared, and riding with her servant she came towards them. Lord Marston had to admit that the Prince had been right:

she was even more beautiful off the stage than she was on.

Her skin had a translucent clearness and there was, he thought, something very spiritual about her which she portrayed in her dancing.

She wore a blue habit against which her fair hair was the colour of sunshine, but her eyes were a definite green.

The Prince rode his horse alongside hers, and taking her gloved hand raised it to his lips. Then he looked into her eyes and Lord Marston knew that his friend had not exaggerated.

These two people belonged to each other.

"I thought . . . perhaps I should meet . . . you here this . . . morning," Lokita said, making no pretence that she had not been looking forward to it.

"I have been waiting an eternity," the Prince said in his deep voice. "I was afraid you might have changed your mind."

"Miss Anderson wanted me to . . . stay at home and . . . rest," Lokita replied, "but I had to . . . come."

"I was willing you to do so."

The Prince relinquished her hand. Then as if he suddenly remembered his manners he said:

"May I introduce my best friend, Lord Marston? He is an Englishman."

"And, may I add, an admirer who has been spellbound by your dancing," Lord Marston said.

"Thank you," Lokita replied simply.

"I have seen you five times now," Lord Marston went on, "and each time has been more enthralling than the last. Moreover, your dance is always a little different."

"I dance as I feel."

It was what Lord Marston had thought.

No teacher, no Producer, could have designed such movements, such steps, which came, as the Prince would have said, from the soul.

Their horses were restless and they moved forward, riding three abreast with Serge behind them.

The Prince's eyes were on Lokita's face, and as if she could not help herself she kept looking at him and finding it hard to look away.

"Let me come back with you," the Prince said. "I would like to pay my respects to Miss Anderson and hope she is not too distressed by the events of yesterday evening."

"It was very frightening for her," Lokita said, "and for . . . me. She has decided that in the future when we go to the Theatre we will take Serge with us."

She looked back at the man behind her and the Prince followed her glance. Then he said in surprise:

"Your servant looks Russian."

"He is Russian."

"And you?"

There was a little pause before Lokita said:

"My . . . mother was Russian."

"I knew it!" the Prince exclaimed. "I knew there was something not only in our minds and hearts that drew us together, but also in our blood."

He looked at Lord Marston with a smile of triumph.

"Do you see, Hugo? We are both Slavs! That is why we understand each other, and we shall always understand each other, while you often find it difficult!"

"I do not . . . know whether Andy would . . . wish to see you," Lokita said a little hesitatingly, as if she was following the train of her thoughts.

"She would think it very remiss of me and exceedingly ill-mannered if I did not call to enquire after you both," the Prince said. "Besides, I have a suggestion to make."

"What is that?"

"It is that I should give a party for you—for you and Miss Anderson—on Saturday night."

"A . . . party?" Lokita questioned. "I have never been to a party."

"Then mine will be the first," the Prince said with a note of triumph in his voice, "and it will be a new experience."

He and Lokita looked at each other for a moment. Then she said:

"I do not think that . . . Andy will allow me to go to a . . . party."

"I will persuade her," the Prince said confidently, "and it shall be a Russian party."

There was a sudden light in Lokita's eyes.

"Really a Russian party?" she asked.

"Everything about it shall be as Russian as possible," the Prince answered. "We will wear Russian dress and there will be gypsy violins—"

He stopped suddenly.

"It will all be a surprise."

"It sounds too wonderful, too exciting!" Lokita said. "But I am afraid that Andy will say no."

"Leave Miss Anderson to me," the Prince replied firmly.

They galloped their horses, then turned towards the little house on the edge of the Bois.

The Prince had seen it the previous night, and now in the sunshine he thought, as Lord Marston did, that it was as perfect in its small simplicity as Lokita herself.

She rode in through the iron gate and while Serge held their horses Lokita led them inside the house.

There was the scent of lilac and in the little Salon it seemed to Lord Marston that every possible table was decorated with vases of flowers.

Miss Anderson was sitting writing at her desk, but when Lokita entered with the two men behind her she rose to her feet.

Lord Marston watching her closely thought there was an expression of horror on her face.

Then courteously she greeted both the Prince and himself and asked them to sit down.

"We were on our way to call on you, Miss Anderson," the Prince said, "when we met Miss Lawrence riding with her servant. I am delighted to see that she has suffered no ill effects from the events of last night, and I am hoping that you can say the same."

"I am quite well, thank you, Your Highness," Miss Anderson said in a somewhat repressed tone.

The Prince engaged her in conversation as he had done the previous evening, and although Miss Anderson responded politely, Lord Marston had the idea that she was exerting a rigid control over herself.

There were, he was sure, deep reservations behind the commonplace remarks they were exchanging.

Lokita said nothing. She only sat, looking exceedingly beautiful, listening to the conversation.

"I have an invitation to offer you," the Prince said to Miss Anderson, "which I very much hope you will accept."

She did not reply but her lips tightened for a moment.

"It is," he went on, "that you and Miss Lawrence should after the Theatre on Saturday night permit me to give a party for you in my garden."

"While appreciating the kindness of your invitation, Your Highness, I regret that we must refuse," Miss Anderson replied.

For the first time since they had sat down Lokita made a little sound, and it was almost a cry of pain.

The Prince, who had been looking only at Miss Anderson, now turned and as their eyes met it was all too obvious to anyone watching what they felt for each other.

Then with an effort the Prince turned again to the Englishwoman and said in his most beguiling voice:

"I cannot take no for an answer. Miss Lawrence tells me she has never been to a party. I am prepared to give you any sort of party you choose, but I think that she would like it to be a Russian one."

"A Russian party, Andy!" Lokita interposed. "Think how exciting that would be! We have talked of them so often and I have read about them in books, but it is not the same as being present at one."

"No, of course it is not," the Prince agreed, "and so, Miss Anderson, please give your consent. As Miss Lawrence can rest on Sunday, it will not be too tiring for her."

Miss Anderson seemed to be thinking seriously, and Lord Marston watching her was aware that she was tense. Then she said slowly:

"It is difficult, Your Highness, to refuse your kindness."

Lokita jumped to her feet.

"That means we can go! Oh, Andy, how wonderful! I was afraid . . . so desperately afraid that you meant to refuse."

Her eyes were like a child's sparkling with excitement as she said to the Prince:

"It will really be Russian, just as if we were not in Paris but in St. Petersburg or Moscow?"

"Or on my own Estate," the Prince finished. "I promise you it will be completely authentic."

"Oh, thank you . . . thank you!"

She looked lovely and in her excitement she put out her hands towards the Prince impulsively, then dropped them suddenly.

The Prince was once again addressing Miss Anderson.

"If you will permit me to do so, I would like to send you and Miss Lawrence Russian costumes to wear at my party," he said. "I will have them conveyed to the Theatre so that you can change into them there, and my carriage will bring you straight to my house."

As if he sensed Miss Anderson's hesitation, he said insistently:

"You would feel embarrassed, I am sure, wearing fancy dress driving in a hired *fiacre*."

"Yes, of course," Miss Anderson agreed. "You think of everything, Your Highness."

"I try to," the Prince said.

As if having gained his objective he knew it would be a mistake to overstay his welcome, the Prince said good-bye to Miss Anderson, then to Lokita.

Lord Marston was aware that as he touched her hand it was as if a tremor went through them both and there was a sudden magnetism in the air that was inescapable.

Hastily he made some remarks to Miss Anderson to try to distract her from what was happening.

As she replied in her calm, sensible voice, he thought she had not observed anything unusual.

As the Prince rode away with Lord Marston he said:

"Saturday! It is a hell of a long time ahead, Hugo!"

"You can see her in the Bois," Lord Marston replied.

"I do not know if it is wise," the Prince answered.

"Wise?"

"I am afraid of that woman. I do not know why, but I have the feeling that she is a dangerous antagonist."

Lord Marston laughed.

"You are exaggerating, Ivan! She seems pleasant enough to me. After all, it is obvious that neither she not Lokita has really any affinity for the stage. In fact it seems extraordinary, now that I have met Lokita, that she should ever have entertained for one moment a stage career."

"Something which will speedily come to an end as soon as she is with me," the Prince said, and added fiercely: "How do you think I can bear to have other men looking at her? People being able to pay money to see her dance?"

"You wish to shut her up in a harem?" Lord Marston questioned.

"That is exactly what I want!" the Prince replied. "I want her to myself, entirely and completely. I want to be alone with her, without the interference or intervention of anyone."

He sighed, then he added:

"If I had any real sense I would kidnap her and take her off to a deserted island or to some far-off part of the earth where no-one would ever find us."

"Ivan—for God's sake!" Lord Marston ejaculated. "That is something that not even you can do! I am quite certain that if you attempted anything of the sort Miss Anderson would have the Police on your heels within ten minutes of your departure."

"That is what prevents me from doing what I really wish," the Prince said. "I have no desire for Lokita to be embroiled in any scandal."

"And what you suggest would be an international one," Lord Marston said. "Her mother may have been Russian, but I am prepared to bet a large sum of money that her father was English."

"Why not?" the Prince asked carelessly. "She does not look English, but her hair is fair and Lawrence is certainly an English name."

"She is also undoubtedly a lady," Lord Marston added. "In which case, why all this secrecy? Why has she never been to a party? Why is she allowed to speak to no-one at the Theatre?"

He paused before he said:

"I am also prepared to bet, Ivan, that Lawrence is not her real name."

"Why should you think that?" the Prince queried.

"Because like you I am being intuitive," Lord Marston answered. "Dammit all, the whole set-up is mysterious and in fact very un-English."

"I do not think we shall get anywhere by asking questions," the Prince said.

"I am quite certain of that," Lord Marston agreed. "That woman, who I imagine is Lokita's Governess, is, I am sure, as closed as a clam. We shall get nothing out of her."

"Leave it to me," the Prince said confidently.

"I know exactly what you are thinking," Lord Marston said with a smile. "You are convinced, in your usual modest way, that there is not a woman alive, whatever her age, whatever her nationality, whom you cannot eventually twist round your little finger."

"How well you know me, Hugo" the Prince said mockingly; then he spurred his horse and there was no time for further conversation.

As Lord Marston had half-expected, they did not meet Lokita again in the Bois.

Every morning they went to the spot where they had encountered her before, and when she did not turn up they looked for her in every other possible place, only to be frustrated.

By Friday the Prince could stand it no more and called at the house.

The door was opened by an elderly French woman who dropped a curtsey at the sight of the two gentlemen.

"Is Miss Anderson at home?" the Prince asked.

"*Non, Monsieur,* Miss Anderson and Miss Lokita are out driving."

"They are both well?"

"Very well, *Monsieur.*"

"Please tell Miss Anderson that I am greatly looking forward to seeing them both tomorrow evening at my party, that as arranged the costumes will be sent to the Theatre, and that my carriage will be waiting for them after the performance."

"I will give the ladies your message, *Monsieur,*" the maid replied.

There seemed nothing else the Prince could say, but just as he was turning away he said:

"I hope both ladies received the flowers I sent them."

"Beautiful flowers have arrived every day, *Monsieur,*" the maid answered.

"And they pleased the ladies?"

"*M'mselle* Lokita loves flowers, *Monsieur.* She was thrilled with the bowl of orchids that arrived yesterday."

"I am extremely gratified that she liked them" the Prince said.

"Are you wise?" Lord Marston asked as they rode away. "You will frighten the Dragon if you try to tempt them with expensive gifts as you did before."

"I have learnt my lesson," the Prince answered. "The orchids were merely in a crystal bowl arranged by a master hand, and for every flower that Lokita has received, Miss Anderson's have equalled if not surpassed hers."

"You are beginning to have a little common sense," Lord Marston said approvingly.

"Those I sent to Lokita conveyed a message which only she could understand," the Prince added.

He said no more, but as soon as they returned home he busied himself with preparing for the party, which Lord Marston realised was to be as fantastic and extravagant as those he had seen in Russia.

He could understand that if it was anything like the parties in the Royal Palaces of St. Petersburg, Lokita would find it astounding.

To him as a young man, the colours of the Palaces alone had seemed fantastic.

The Youssoupov Palace, which was yellow, was reflected in the Fontanka Canal; the Voronzov Palace overlooking the Neva was crimson and white; the Taivride Palace was a rich blue. Others were in lilac or salmon pink.

When he had been in St. Petersburg, the Winter Palace of the Tsar, which had originally been coloured pistachio green with white and gold pillars, had been repainted maroon red.

When the city with the first heavy snows in November was transformed into a white and sparkling world, the brilliant colours of the Palaces had brought a fairy-like appearance to the whole place.

Then there had been the jingling and tinkling of silver bells as people in their sleighs sped over the snows and ice from Palace to Palace to enjoy the fantastic parties that were given night after night.

Thirty thousand candles shone in huge crystal chandeliers in the Winter Palace, or were arranged spirally round the jasper pillars bordering the Ball-Room.

Everywhere gigantic mirrors reflected the jewels that sparkled and shimmered as ladies who wore them danced to the music of innumerable violins.

Resplendent *Aides-de-camp* swung round the polished floors with beautiful women who wore necklaces down to their waists, *rivières* of diamonds, yards of pearls, and brooches of rubies and emeralds as big as pigeons' eggs.

The supper-tables were set with gold dishes festooned with garlands of hot-house flowers, and delicacies travelled thousands of miles from other parts of the world to tempt the jaded palates of the guests.

At the Balls which Lord Marston had attended, the Ladies-in-Waiting, following the example of the Empress, wore their traditional Court dresses of richly coloured velvets with ermine trimming and splendid jewels to match the velvet.

There were parures of rubies for crimson velvet, sapphires for blue, and emeralds for green, and the variety of brilliant uniforms worn by the Russian officers ranged the whole spectrum of colour, including even pink and violet.

There were gypsies to sing and play, and their music grew wilder and wilder as the night wore on. No-one gave a thought, Lord Marston knew, to the poor who watched outside in the bitter, freezing cold, their feet wrapped in birch bark and rags.

That at least was one thing that would be missing in Paris, Lord Marston told himself as he watched with amusement the Prince's plans for what he thought of as "Lokita's Russian Party."

The whole of the huge garden at the Château was to be covered in white—the artificial snow having an advantage over the real thing in that it did not freeze the feet.

Fir trees were planted in the ground to furnish the dark, impenetrable background of the Russian woods, and pools were constructed of mirrors to look like ice, while real *troikas* were there for those who wished to drive in them.

Gypsies, many of them genuine Russian gypsies, were summoned from all parts of France, and Russian choirs were paid to break engagements so that they could sing the haunting love-songs that were so essentially a part of Russian festivities.

Lord Marston knew that here the Prince was bound to deviate a little from reality, for nearly all Russian songs were sad and melancholy, the songs of those who had lost their loves and who would in consequence suffer and die.

The songs were part of the suffering endured by the Russians for generations and were sung accompanied by the balalaika and the accordion.

They echoed over the rolling wheat-fields and the Steppes, across the sunflower plantations of the Ukraine, and in the snow-bound winter darkness of the north.

As always when the Prince was occupied, he concentrated on what he was doing to the exclusion of all else.

Lord Marston found it difficult to tempt him out even to luncheon or dinner in one of the fashionable restaurants, and when they talked of subjects which had always interested them the Prince's mind kept returning to the party, and of course to Lokita.

"I want to see her face as she steps into the garden and sees the picture of Russia as she must always have imagined it."

"Perhaps she will want to dance," Lord Marston suggested.

The Prince turned on him violently.

"The people whom I have engaged will dance for

her," he reflected. "She will not give anything of herself to them. I will not allow it!"

Every night the Prince and Lord Marston went to the Theatre to watch Lokita, and when they came away Lord Marston was aware that each time he saw her the Prince grew deeper and deeper in love.

It seemed to consume him like a burning fire so that at times Lord Marston felt it might break every restraint and the last vestige of civilisation would fall away from him.

It was inevitable that it should make him look more handsome, more compelling, and at the same time more authoritative.

He was like a man who was fighting a hard battle but believed that victory was in sight.

He spoke of himself as a suppliant at Lokita's feet, but Lord Marston knew that really he was a conqueror who would gain the height of his ambition—the zenith of his desires.

Because of the Prince's impatience, he too felt as if it took unusually long for the days to pass until Saturday.

When it came, the morning was clear and sunny and the Prince came into his room early to say:

"It is a good omen, the sun is in the sky, there is not a cloud to be seen. Come and look at the garden."

Dozens of men were spreading the artifical snow on the ground and on the trees. There were others erecting false bonfires which glowed beneath great logs of wood with crimson rags which fluttered between them as if they were flames.

It was all amazingly and unbelievably lovely and Lord Marston thought that no woman who appreciated beauty, especially Lokita, could fail to be thrilled by it.

The Prince supervised every detail. Then before they were packed up to be taken to the Theatre he showed Lord Marston the Russian gowns he had chosen for Lokita and Miss Anderson to wear.

They were the colourful and attractive traditional

costumes that had been a part of Russian history since the first Romanovs in the seventeenth century, who, realising that their people expected pomp and circumstance, had bedecked themselves with jewels until they appeared to be covered with them.

The head-dress for Miss Anderson was made of pearls, and there were strings of them which would fall from round her chin to below her waist.

Lokita's was more delicate and only as he looked at the jewels worked into the embroidery on the skirt and bodice of her gown did Lord Marston exclaim:

"Surely, Ivan, those are real emeralds and diamonds?"

"But of course!" the Prince replied. "Do you think I would offer Lokita anything that was imitation?"

"But diamonds—just for a party!" Lord Marston expostulated. "Besides, they may be dropped or stolen."

"Nothing will be stolen from Lokita while she is with me," the Prince said firmly.

The guests had all been asked to come in Russian costume, and as there was nothing that Parisians enjoyed more than dressing up, Lord Marston knew that everyone would be only too delighted to oblige their host.

"Do you intend to invite the Emperor and Empress?" Lord Marston enquired as the invitations were despatched by hand.

"I could not stand the boredom of their presence," the Prince replied, "but I have asked the Prince Napoleon."

The Prince was the most controversial and at the same time the most popular man in all France.

He disliked the Empress and assumed a frank independence of the Emperor.

His private life was as controversial as his public life. His behaviour towards his mistresses was legendary and he flaunted them in full view of all Paris.

The Prince had married seven years ago, but it was a purely political arrangement intended to unite

France and Italy, and no two people could have been more unsuited to each other.

It was therefore not surprising that marriage did not modify the Prince's immorality.

It was said openly that there was always some petticoat lying about his bed-room in the morning. However, because he was so witty and such an excellent guest, and had a charm *par excellence,* no party in Paris was complete without him.

"I wonder what the Prince Napoleon will think of Lokita when he meets her," Lord Marston said. "I heard that he invited her out to supper but his invitations were refused."

"As mine were," the Prince said, "which is why I had to employ other tactics."

"And very reprehensible ones," Lord Marston added with severity. "I wonder what Lokita will say when she learns the truth."

"That depends on whether I ever tell her," the Prince replied, then added almost angrily:

"But she would forgive me! She would forgive me because she loves me. Do not forget that—she loves me!"

Lord Marston thought that was true, and yet inevitably his mind went to Miss Anderson.

Surely she would have something to say about this liaison, because it could be nothing more between the charge she had guarded so assiduously and the Prince.

Because he was so excited and so anxious about the evening, the Prince was dressed far earlier than was necessary and came into Lord Marston's bed-room to hurry him.

He was arrayed in his regimental uniform and looked so impressive and at the same time so fantastically attractive that Lord Marston thought it would be hard for any girl, let alone one as inexperienced as Lokita, not to fall head-over-heels in love with him.

"Do hurry, Hugo!" the Prince admonished.

"You are very impatient, Ivan," Lord Marston replied good-humouredly.

"I want to be quite certain that dinner is finished and everyone is out in the garden by the time Lokita arrives."

"There is no likelihood of her being here until nearly twelve o'clock," Lord Marston said soothingly.

"You know how long these meals take," the Prince replied.

That was true, since over two hundred people were being entertained in what was usually used as the Ball-Room.

Because it was to be a Russian evening, Tokay, which was the fashionable drink in St. Petersburg, was to be offered to the guests as well as the best French champagne.

The Prince's Chefs were determined to produce a menu which would be the envy of every other host in Paris, besides which there was to be a completely Russian supper after Lokita arrived for those who were still hungry after the gargantuan dinner.

Looking at the brilliant scene in the Dining-Room a few hours later, Lord Marston thought that the Prince had achieved his object and really had rivalled the splendour of the Winter Palace.

Outside, the garden was an enchantment.

It was fairy-tale Russia as everybody imagined it to be, without the cruelty, the starvation, the poor, and the oppressed.

Russia as she existed only in the hearts of those who loved her, and yet because it had a mystery and beauty of its own it was inescapably lovely.

Lord Marston enjoyed himself.

He had a great many friends amongst the Prince's guests and a number of women who were so attractive that he thought they might well encourage him to prolong his visit to Paris.

It was only later, in the garden, when the Prince came to stand beside him that he realised the time.

"She has not arrived!" the Prince said in a low voice.

Lord Marston drew his gold watch from his waist-coat pocket. The hands pointed almost to one o'clock.

"Perhaps the performance ran late," he suggested.

"She does not wait for the end, as you well know," the Prince replied.

Lord Marston with a muttered apology left the lady to whom he had been talking and walked with the Prince towards the house, their feet crunching on the artificial snow.

"Something has happened—something has prevented her from coming," the Prince said in a tortured voice. "It must be the doing of that damned woman!"

"She agreed to the party," Lord Marston said.

"Then why is Lokita not here? I told the carriage to be outside the stage-door at eleven o'clock. One of my most trusted men was on the box."

"There must be some reasonable explanation," Lord Marston said soothingly. "She should be here at any moment. Relax, Ivan, and have a drink."

They entered the Salon and he put a glass of champagne into the Prince's hand as he spoke.

The Prince took one sip, then with a violent gesture dashed the crystal glass into the fireplace.

"She is not coming. I know she is not coming!" he cried. "God, Hugo, if I should lose her!"

Lord Marston looked at his watch again. It did seem rather ominous. They walked into the hall, and as they did so one of the flunkeys who was standing at the doorway turned to exclaim:

"Here is the carriage!"

The Prince's look of despair vanished. He hurried forward.

He was on the steps as the coachman drew the horses to a standstill.

The footmen ran down to open the carriage door,

but as they did so Lord Marston saw that there was
no-one inside.

A Russian servant jumped down from the box and
came towards the Prince.

"What has happened? Where are the ladies I sent
you to collect?" the Prince asked furiously.

"They came out of the Theatre, Your Highness,
shortly after eleven-thirty."

"And you were waiting for them?"

"Yes, Your Highness, but as they got into the carriage they asked if we would take them first to the
railway station."

"To the railway station?" the Prince repeated in a
strangled voice.

"Yes, Your Highness. They said they had to say
good-bye to someone who was leaving by train."

"And you did as they asked?"

"Yes, Your Highness."

"And when you got there?"

"The ladies alighted, Your Highness, and went into the station."

"They had luggage with them?"

"No, Your Highness, only a hat-box."

Lord Marston drew in his breath.

Already he guessed what the hat-box contained.

"Go on!" the Prince said testily.

"I asked if I should carry the hat-box for the ladies, Your Highness, but they refused and I saw waiting
for them just inside the station a man and a woman
with a pile of luggage."

"A man and a woman," the Prince repeated. "A
tall man—a servant? A Russian?"

"I think so, Your Highness."

The Prince did not speak and the man continued:

"They moved away, and we waited for an hour,
Your Highness."

Still the Prince did not reply and the servant continued:

"I then thought that something must be wrong and

went into the station to investigate. Several trains had come and gone while we were waiting outside, and now there were only a few passengers still in the station—the two ladies were not among them."

"You were certain of that?"

"Quite certain, Your Highness, and I made enquiries of a porter."

"What did he say?"

"He said he was almost certain he had seen the four people I described boarding a train which had left shortly after midnight."

"Did he say where it was going?"

"He was not absolutely certain, Your Highness, but he thought it was the express to Calais."

The Prince stood immobile. Then the servant who had opened the carriage door drew something from the inside.

Lord Marston saw that he held in his arms two Russian costumes, one of them embroidered with real jewels!

Chapter Five

Lokita stood looking out onto the small Square.

There was a garden in the centre of it, but the trees seemed grey and somehow lifeless compared with those in Paris.

The sky was overcast and she felt that London was in fact all grey, dull, and dismal, like the despair in her heart.

She was thinner than she had been a week ago and there were dark lines under her eyes because every night she had wept until she was exhausted.

She had wept for the Prince, for her lost dreams, for missing the Russian party he had arranged for her, and because she felt that the future held nothing but loneliness.

She had hardly believed that she was hearing aright when Andy had told her they were leaving for London that very night.

She had come off the stage to the tumultuous applause of the audience with her eyes alight and a rising excitement within her at the thought of the evening that lay ahead.

All day she had been unable to talk of anything else.

"Prince Ivan has said that his garden will look like

Russia, Andy," she had said. "Do you think he will have snow on the ground, and if so, what will it be made of?"

"It is not always snowing in Russia," Miss Anderson had replied in a voice that sounded as if the words were dragged from her. "In the south it can be very hot, and there is sunshine and flowers."

"You told me about that before," Lokita replied, "but I always think of sleighs moving over the snow and the domes and spires of St. Petersburg gleaming gold against the sky. Papa used to describe it to me."

Miss Anderson did not answer, and Lokita had thought that she was reluctant to go to the party because she would meet people there, and she had never been allowed to make friends.

"I am interested in no-one except the . . . Prince," Lokita whispered to herself.

She had run ahead of Miss Anderson up the iron staircase to her dressing-room, knowing that the Russian costumes the Prince had promised to deliver at the Theatre would be waiting.

They were lying on the arm-chair and she gave a cry of sheer delight when she saw them.

"Look, Andy, how beautiful they are!" she exclaimed. But to her astonishment Miss Anderson said harshly:

"Change into the clothes in which you came."

"But why, Andy? It was arranged that we should dress here and go straight to the party."

"Do as I say," Miss Anderson commanded.

"I want to wear my Russian gown," Lokita protested. "How can I go to the party without it? It is so beautiful!"

"Put on your ordinary clothes."

There was something in the way she spoke that made Lokita look at Miss Anderson apprehensively.

There was a silence. Then she said in a voice hardly above a whisper:

"What are you . . . saying?"

"We are leaving for London tonight!"

"For London? But . . . why?"

"Because we can no longer stay here in Paris."

"Why? Why?" Lokita demanded.

Because she had obeyed Miss Anderson all her life, she was soon dressed in her ordinary clothes, which were covered by her velvet cape.

Then they went down the iron stairs to the stage-door.

Miss Anderson also wore a cloak, and it was only when they had stepped into the Prince's carriage and the servants had been told to take them to the railway station that Lokita realised that Miss Anderson had brought the Russian costumes with her.

She drew them from their place of concealment, and as she did so Lokita noticed that there was also a hat-box.

"What is in that?" she asked.

"Our bonnets," Miss Anderson replied uncompromisingly. "I do not wish the Prince's servants to know what we are doing until we have actually left Paris."

There was nothing Lokita could do, nothing she could say. When finally the train for Calais had steamed out of the station, she had shut her eyes to prevent the tears from running down her cheeks.

She had no wish to cry in front of other people, but at night when she was alone she had wept until her pillow was wet.

Miss Anderson had expected to stay with her sister, who was married to a Dr. Edwards, who practised in Islington; but when they arrived they found that the house was too small for extra visitors.

Mrs. Edwards had found them accommodation in a Boarding-House which was practically next door.

It was small and not very comfortable, but Lokita was too distressed to feel anything but an inescapable sense of loss.

"What will the Prince think?" she kept asking herself.

How could he ever understand that she had no wish to be rude or to hurt him by leaving as she had been forced to do?

On their third day in London Miss Anderson became ill.

Her brother-in-law examined her and said gravely that it was imperative that Miss Anderson should see a Specialist.

"We cannot afford it!" she answered firmly, but he insisted.

Now Lokita was waiting for the verdict of Sir George Lester, of whom Dr. Edwards had spoken with awe and admiration.

Lokita could not really believe that there was anything seriously wrong with Andy. She had always been so strong and indestructible.

It was only in the last month or two in Paris that she had been too tired to walk in the Bois as she had always liked to in the past, and sometimes when they left the Theatre she had seemed as they drove home too exhausted even to speak.

The door opened behind Lokita and she turned round as Sir George Lester came into the room.

He looked grave and her eyes were apprehensive as she waited for him to speak.

"I have examined Miss Anderson," he said quietly, "who I understand is your Guardian."

Lokita nodded.

"I think you would want me to be frank and tell you the truth," he went on.

"Is Andy . . . very ill?"

Lokita could not help the question bursting from her lips.

"Yes, my dear, very ill!" Sir George Lester replied. "Her heart is affected, and there are also other complications with which I need not distress you."

"What can we do? How can she be cured?" Lokita asked.

Sir George shook his head.

"I have told Miss Anderson that she must rest. She must not be agitated or upset by anything or anybody. I have given her certain drops which she must always have by her to take if she is in pain or appears on the verge of collapse."

Lokita drew in her breath.

She was very pale and now her eyes were frightened.

"Is there . . . nothing more we can . . . do?" she asked almost in a whisper.

"She is worried about you, my child," Sir George said, "and therefore you must do everything in your power to reassure her, to keep her from being distressed."

"I will do that," Lokita promised.

"I am sure that is half the battle," Sir George said kindly.

He patted Lokita on the arm and turned to leave the room, picking up his top-hat from where he had left it just inside the door.

Dr. Edwards was waiting outside for him and Lokita heard the men talking to each other in low voices as they went downstairs.

She ran into Miss Anderson's room.

It was a very small bed-room, inadequately furnished, and Miss Anderson was lying propped against a number of pillows on a narrow brass bedstead.

Lokita forced herself to walk slowly to her side.

"Andy!" she said with a little throb in her voice. "Oh, Andy!"

"It is all right, dear," Miss Anderson replied. "Doctors always make a great fuss over nothing. I shall just take it easy, then I will be all right. You can be sure of that."

Lokita could not speak for fear that she would burst

into tears. Then in a different tone of voice, as if she did not wish to be overheard, Miss Anderson said:

"Send for Serge. I want to speak to him."

"Yes, of course," Lokita agreed. "I will find him."

She left the room and found, as she expected, that Serge was hovering on the stairs with Marie beside him.

They were both desperately anxious to know the doctor's verdict.

"Miss Anderson wants to speak to you, Serge," Lokita said, and without a word the Russian went towards Miss Anderson's bed-room.

"What did the doctor say about *Madame?*" Marie asked in French.

Lokita drew her into the Sitting-Room which was used by all the guests staying at the Lodging-House and told her what Sir George had said.

"We must look after *Madame,*" Marie agreed. "It was too much for her, rushing away from Paris in that crazy manner! This place is uncomfortable, and the food . . . !"

She made a face which was more expressive than any words.

"I know," Lokita answered. "Perhaps we could convince her that we should all go home."

As she spoke she knew that Andy would never agree to return to Paris as long as the Prince was there.

They were hiding from him, and the one place he was most unlikely to look, Lokita knew, was in Islington.

She heard Serge come out of Miss Anderson's bed-room and go down the stairs.

She looked at Marie.

"I wonder where Andy has sent him."

She went back into the bed-room.

Miss Anderson's eyes were closed as she entered the room but she opened them as Lokita approached the bed and smiled.

"Where have you sent Serge?" Lokita enquired.

"To find out if Lord Marston is in London," Andy replied.

* * *

Lord Marston was sitting in the library of his house in Curzon Street, opening a huge pile of letters that he had found on his return from Paris.

Although he had been back for several days, the pile seemed undiminished and he knew it was because he had little time to give to his correspondence while the Prince was staying with him.

When he discovered that Lokita had been spirited away, the Prince had behaved like a madman, and it was with the greatest difficulty that Lord Marston restrained him from doing anything wild or desperate.

"I have lost her! God, Hugo, I have lost her!" the Prince had exclaimed over and over again.

He had refused to return to the party but had there and then driven to Lokita's house near the Bois.

There the Prince had hammered on the door until, frightened and apprehensive, a middle-aged caretaker had come downstairs with a coat over his nightshirt to find out what was happening.

The Prince had cross-questioned him, but it was obvious that the man knew very little.

He and his wife, he explained, had been asked by Marie, who was their niece, to look after the house as the ladies were going away.

"Where have they gone?" the Prince asked fiercely.

The man shrugged his shoulders.

"Is it to England?"

He considered the question, then replied that he thought it was. He had heard his niece say they would want thick clothes because she was sure it was always cold in London.

The Prince looked at Lord Marston.

"London!" he exclaimed.

But that was the only information he could obtain.

Marie had not confided in her relatives and Lord Marston thought it was doubtful whether Miss Anderson had told anybody where she intended to stay.

It was obvious that she had planned their precipitate departure carefully and, Lord Marston was inclined to think, had kept it from Lokita until the very last moment.

One thing they learnt under the Prince's continued cross-examination of the caretaker was that Miss Anderson had sold a valuable ikon.

The caretaker's wife had heard Marie say to Miss Anderson:

"*M'mselle* loves that ikon. It means something very special to her. She will be upset to lose it."

"There is no reason why she should know that it has been sold," Miss Anderson had replied sharply.

The Prince had guessed who was the most likely buyer in Paris of valuable ikons. He and Lord Marston had gone there the following morning to buy it back, doubtless at double what the man had paid for it.

Nevertheless, it had been something of Lokita's for the Prince to treasure.

He had then decided that they must leave for London, giving Lord Marston hardly time to inform the British Ambassador of his intention before they were in the train and rushing toward the coast.

When they reached London even the Prince realised it was not going to be easy to find two ladies without any idea where they might have hidden themselves.

At this very moment Lord Marston knew, as he slit open another letter, that the Prince was engaging private detectives to search every possible area of the city.

It was a quest which was bound to be considerably handicapped by the fact that there were no pictures either of Miss Anderson or of Lokita to help their identification.

It seemed hopeless, but at least, Lord Marston thought, the Prince had something with which to occupy himself.

He was suffering from what the Russians describe as *Tosca,* an inner misery, an agony of the soul which is for all Slavs a part of their innate fatalism.

In the Prince's case it was so intense, so pregnant with distress, that at times Lord Marston was afraid he might end his life rather than continue to suffer.

There was no doubt of one thing and that was that he was desperately, overwhelmingly in love.

Lord Marston had in the past seen him infatuated, beguiled, and almost bewitched by women while he was pursuing them, but never before had he known the Prince to be swept off his feet by an emotion that shook from him everything except the elemental depth of his love.

It was as if, Lord Marston thought reflectively, he was no longer a Prince, an aristocrat, the possessor of great wealth and a position of authority, he was just a man.

A man yearning for the unattainable, distraught by the loss of everything that mattered to him, and immersed in the darkness of an overwhelming despair.

"Thank God I have never been in love like that!" Lord Marston said to himself for the hundredth time.

A servant opened the door and he looked up impatiently.

He had no wish to be interrupted as he wished to clear as much as he could of his correspondence before the Prince returned.

"There's a man asking to see you, M'Lord."

"I can see no-one."

"He's very insistent, M'Lord. He says he has a message from a Miss Anderson."

Lord Marston stared at his servant incredulously.

"Did you say—Miss Anderson?"

"Yes, M'Lord."

"Show the man in immediately!"

"Very good, M'Lord."

Lord Marston rose from the desk and was standing by the fireplace when Serge was announced.

The big Russian stood inside the door, twisting his hat in his hands.

"Good-morning, Serge," Lord Marston said calmly.

"Good-day, M'Lord."

"You have a message for me?"

"Yes, M'Lord."

"What is it?"

"Miss Anderson sent me to your house, M'Lord, to find out when you were expected to return from Paris, and to say that when you did arrive she would wish to see you. It is urgent!"

"In which case," Lord Marston replied, "it would be best if you took me to her immediately."

"Very good, M'Lord."

It took only a few minutes for His Lordship's carriage to be brought round from the mews. Lord Marston stepped inside as Serge climbed onto the box beside the coachman.

As they drove off Lord Marston found himself wondering why he had been sent for.

Could anything have happened to Lokita? he wondered. Had there been an accident? If she was dead or injured, he wondered, how it would be possible to break the news to the Prince?

He spent the whole journey turning over in his mind the extraordinary circumstances which must have compelled Miss Anderson to send for him.

When the carriage drew up outside the shabby Lodging-House in Islington Square, he thought as he stepped out onto the pavement that it was far from the right setting for Lokita.

He formed a similar impression as he saw her waiting for him just inside the small dark hall.

She held out both her hands and he saw the gladness in her eyes.

"You have come with Serge!" she exclaimed. "Andy was not certain if you would have returned to London."

"The Prince and I came back the day after you left us," Lord Marston explained.

He saw the expression in Lokita's eyes when he mentioned the Prince, and he knew without being told that she was suffering in the same way that he was.

"Andy is ill," Lokita told him as they went up the stairs. "She has seen an important doctor, Sir George Lester, who said she is not to be upset and we all have to do . . . everything she . . . wants."

They went for a few more steps before Lokita added:

"Sir George said it was her heart, and I am afraid . . . terribly afraid that something might . . . happen to her."

Lord Marston understood what she meant.

Lokita opened a door.

"Lord Marston is here, Andy," she said. "May I bring him in?"

"Show him in, Lokita, and I wish to see him alone," Miss Anderson replied.

Her voice, Lord Marston noticed, still had the undeniable ring of authority.

Lokita smiled at him and he walked into the bedroom.

"I am sorry to hear you are ill, Miss Anderson," he said.

There was a hard chair by the bed and he sat down on it.

"I sent Serge to find you, Lord Marston," Miss Anderson replied, "because I need your help."

"You know I will do anything that is within my power," Lord Marston replied.

"I have not long to live," Miss Anderson said.

Lord Marston would have expostulated, but she brushed his words aside, saying:

"I made the doctors tell me the truth, something they are invariably reluctant to do; but I am a dying woman, and now I am only concerned about Lokita."

"Of course," Lord Marston murmured.

"There is no-one else I can trust except you," Miss Anderson said. "Therefore, Lord Marston, I am asking if you will marry her!"

Lord Marston stiffened in sheer astonishment and Miss Anderson went on:

"For the moment, her background must remain a secret and I cannot reveal who she is. All I can tell you, on my most sacred word of honour, is that by breeding she is your equal."

She paused before she added:

"One day you will be able to know the truth of who she is and where she comes from, but for the moment I ask you to trust me and make her your wife."

Her voice died away but her eyes were on Lord Marston's face.

After a moment he said:

"I will be honest, Miss Anderson, and say that I never imagined for one moment that I should receive such a strange suggestion, nor had I thought of Lokita, beautiful though she is, as belonging to me."

He drew in his breath before he went on:

"I think she is in love with Prince Ivan Volkonski, and he is wildly, passionately in love with her."

"I am aware of that," Miss Anderson said sharply, "but you know as well as I do, Lord Marston, that he cannot marry her."

Lord Marston did not speak and Miss Anderson went on:

"I have lived in Russia. As the Prince's mother was a Romanov, he could only marry with permission from the Tsar."

There was a touch of irony in her voice as she added:

"The Tsar, as we both know, would not give his permission for the Prince to marry a young woman who has not only appeared on the stage but about whom there is nothing to prove her parentage."

"And you think this would not count with me?" Lord Marston asked.

"You are English, and Lokita's father was English. She is also beautiful not only in her face but in her character. I confidently believe that if you marry her you will come to love her very deeply."

"And you think she might come to love me?" Lord Marston asked.

Miss Anderson closed her eyes.

As she lay back against her pillows Lord Marston realised for the first time how frail she looked and how different from when he had last seen her in Paris.

Then she had seemed to merit being nicknamed "the Dragon," for there had been a force and a fire about her which had been almost intimidating.

Now she was nothing but a sick woman, old—older than he had thought her to be—and her face was lined not only with age but with suffering.

Because of what Lokita had told him, Lord Marston said quickly:

"Will you give me time to think over what you have proposed? I will send you a message this afternoon or this evening."

Almost as if she had not heard him, Miss Anderson said as she opened her eyes:

"I want you to marry Lokita at once by Special Licence! She must be safe—she must be!"

"I understand," Lord Marston said soothingly, "and I promise you I will give it my most serious consideration."

He rose to his feet as he spoke.

Only as he reached the door did Miss Anderson speak again, and as if with an effort.

"There is—no-one I can—trust except you, and Lokita must be—safe!"

* * *

The Prince was waiting for Lord Marston when he returned. He was standing by the window, staring with unseeing eyes into the garden, and at a glance as he came in through the door Lord Marston knew that his meeting with the detectives had not been encouraging.

They would take his money, that was inevitable, but he was quite sure that to safeguard their own reputations they would have informed the Prince that he set them a task in which they were unlikely to be successful.

Lord Marston walked across the room to stand in front of the mantelpiece.

"I have something to tell you, Ivan."

"What is it?" the Prince asked without turning.

"I have just seen Lokita!"

The Prince swung round.

His expression was that of a man who suddenly steps from a dark dungeon into the light.

"You—have—seen—Lokita?"

There was a pause between each word, as if he could hardly say them.

"Miss Anderson sent for me—she is very ill."

The Prince waited.

"She asked me if, to keep Lokita safe, I would marry her."

"Marry her?" the Prince ejaculated; then fiercely, his voice ringing out, he cried:

"If you touch Lokita—if you lay a finger on her —I will kill you!"

"I have not said that I agreed to do so," Lord Marston replied.

"I will keep Lokita safe. I will look after her and worship her for the rest of her life."

"But you cannot offer her marriage."

The Prince was silent.

"Miss Anderson knows that," Lord Marston went on. "She told me she was well aware that you could not marry anybody without the permission of the

Tsar, but she admitted that Lokita is in love with you."

The Prince walked across the room to stand beside Lord Marston.

"I must see Lokita—I must talk to her."

"Are you prepared to ask her if she will become your mistress?" Lord Marston questioned.

The Prince put his hand up to his forehead.

"Mistress or wife—I will love her as no woman has ever been loved before."

"That is not the point, as you well know," Lord Marston said, "and quite frankly, Ivan, I think she is so pure and innocent that she would refuse the only position you can offer her."

The Prince walked across the room and back again then he said in a resolute tone:

"In which case Lokita must not know what we are doing."

"What do you mean by that?" Lord Marston asked.

"I am thinking it out," the Prince said. "You will agree to marry Lokita. You will bring her here and she will marry me—"

"She cannot do that," Lord Marston interrupted.

"If we tell Lokita it will be a Civic Marriage such as is possible in England, and that later I will get the permission of the Tsar for a Church Service, she will believe me," the Prince said.

"A Civic Marriage?" Lord Marston repeated.

"It will be like the type of ceremony which takes place in France in front of the Mayor," the Prince said impatiently. "A few words and the bridal couple are married. Anybody could play that part."

"You intend to deceive Lokita by a bogus ceremony?"

"I intend to ensure that she is safe for life and that she will be loved and protected."

Lord Marston did not speak and the Prince went on:

"I will settle a fortune on her—any sum you like. That will be part of the 'Marriage Contract.' "

He looked at Lord Marston and said angrily:

"Good God, Hugo, you must see it is the only possible way to solve this problem! I love Lokita, she loves me, but for the moment we cannot be married. Perhaps later—who knows—I may be able to persuade the Tsar."

"Miss Anderson assured me her breeding is the equal of my own," Lord Marston said, "but even that may not be enough for you."

"Do you think it matters to me who her parents or her ancestors were?" the Prince asked angrily. "She may come from the gutter or from the steps of the throne. She is Lokita! She is mine! That is the only thing you and I have to consider."

Lord Marston sighed.

"I admit, much as I admire Lokita, much as I feel for her in her present situation, I have no wish to marry any woman who is in love with somebody else."

"Lokita loves me."

The Prince's voice softened as he went on:

"And you know I love her. Her happiness and her future lie in your hands."

"It is too big a responsibility," Lord Marston protested. "Supposing she ever learnt the truth, that she was not in fact married to you? She would denounce you for deceiving her."

"What is the alternative?" the Prince asked practically. "If Miss Anderson dies, are you suggesting that Lokita should go back on the stage without any form of protection?"

Lord Marston did not answer and he went on:

"We know she has no money except what they obtained from the sale of the ikon. Do as I suggest, Hugo. It is the only possible way."

There was silence while the seconds seemed to tick by, then Lord Marston said reluctantly:

"I suppose you are right and there is no alternative."

The Prince gave what was a sound of triumph.

"Write a note immediately and say you will collect Lokita this evening. That will give us time to rehearse someone in the form of Service and draw up the necessary documents with regard to the money I shall settle on her."

He spoke quite quietly, then suddenly he flung his arms above his head and shouted triumphantly:

"We have found her! We have found her, Hugo, and now I have come alive again!"

*   *   *

Driving in Lord Marston's closed carriage, Lokita looked at him with worried eyes.

"Andy said I was to come with you wherever you wish to take me," she said, "but she did not tell me where you were going."

"What else did she tell you?" Lord Marston enquired.

"After your note arrived at luncheon time, it seemed to make her happy, in fact she looked happier than she has ever been since we left Paris."

"What did she say?" he asked.

"She told me that you would collect me at five o'clock and that I was to do exactly what you told me, but she would not tell me what it was."

Lokita's voice sounded even more apprehensive as she added:

"I was . . . frightened because I heard her telling Marie to . . . pack some of my . . . clothes. Am I to stay with you for the . . . night?"

"I think you will stay longer than that," Lord Marston said.

He saw the question in Lokita's expression and added:

"Someone is waiting for you at my house, someone who loves you very much!"

"The . . . Prince!"

Lokita seemed hardly able to breathe the word.

"Yes, the Prince," Lord Marston agreed. "Tell me, Lokita, do you really love him?"

He knew the answer by the light shining in her face before she answered:

"I love him with my whole heart. I have been utterly miserable because I thought I should . . . never see him . . . again."

There was a throb in her voice that was very moving, and Lord Marston put his hand on Lokita's as he said:

"Do you love him enough, Lokita, to deceive Miss Anderson, whom you also love?"

"What do you . . . mean?"

"When I came to see Miss Anderson this morning," Lord Marston answered, "she asked me if I would marry you."

He felt Lokita stiffen in surprise and knew that she had no idea of what had been suggested.

"You are very beautiful, Lokita," Lord Marston went on, "but we both know that you and I are not in love with each other and that you love the Prince."

"I . . . I think he . . . loves me," she murmured.

"He loves you with his whole heart and soul," Lord Marston said. "He has been like a man suffering from a death blow ever since you left Paris, and he thought he would never find you again."

"But now . . . he will . . . marry me?"

"Now he will marry you, but we have to keep it a secret," Lord Marston warned. "You will understand he is a very important person and he should not marry without having first told his family and the Tsar."

"I understand that," Lokita murmured.

"But because Miss Anderson is so ill and because we do not wish to upset her, it would be best for her to think that I have agreed to her proposition and that you and I are to be married this evening."

He felt Lokita's fingers tremble in his, and he knew without asking what she wanted to know.

"Actually," he said quietly, "you will marry the Prince."

"M-marry . . . him?"

The words sounded like a song of joy.

"It will only be a Civic Marriage," Lord Marston explained, "dull and uninspiring. But later, when the Prince has had time to communicate with the Tsar, he hopes it will be possible for you to have the blessing of the Church."

"That is what I would want," Lokita said simply.

"Of course," Lord Marston agreed, "but for the moment, because of the speed with which we have to act, there is no time."

"Do you think . . . that Andy is . . . dying?" Lokita asked hesitatingly.

"She told me she was," Lord Marston replied, "and that is why I am sure you are right and we shouldn't upset her."

"No, of course not," Lokita agreed.

The horses drew up outside Lord Marston's house and he alighted and helped Lokita onto the red carpet which was laid down over the pavement.

They walked across the marble hall, and Lord Marston opened a door to let her enter alone.

The Prince was standing in the middle of the room and Lokita thought as she looked at him that he was more handsome and more compellingly attractive than she remembered.

Their eyes met and for a moment they were neither of them able to move. Then very simply the Prince held out his arms and Lokita ran towards him.

He caught her against him, holding her so tightly that she could feel his heart beating wildly and tumultuously against her breast.

Then he said in a voice that seemed strangled with emotion:

"My darling! My precious! My little *Drouska!* I thought I would never find you again!"

"It was . . . agony leaving . . . you," Lokita whispered.

"But you are here in my arms, and oh, God, how much I love you!"

The Prince looked down at her upturned face, then gently, as if he held himself rigidly under control, he bent his head and his lips found hers.

He kissed her at first with a tenderness which made tears come to her eyes. Then as her lips were soft and yielding beneath his he held her closer still.

Now his kiss became more insistent, more demanding.

It was as if he asked her to give him her heart and drew her soul from her body to make it his.

She felt as if everything beautiful that she had felt in her dancing, everything spiritual that had been close to her when she heard music, was intensified.

It grew in them both until it was like the blazing heat of the sun, and they stood in the centre of it.

It was so compelling, so glorious, so brilliant that she felt as if the light that had blazed out between them blinded her eyes and seeped through her body until they were both swept away by it.

'This is love,' Lokita thought as her whole being responded to his need of her and she felt that every nerve was pulsating with a wonder and joy that was so intense it was almost painful.

"I love you! I love you!"

She wanted to cry the words aloud, she wanted to move, she wanted to dance at the glory and rapture of them.

Still the Prince held her prisoner, captive against him, kissing her with the wild intensity of a man who has come back to life from the dead.

When he raised his head she saw the wonder in his eyes and knew that he felt as she did.

"Is it true that you are here, that you are close to me?" he asked, and his voice was unsteady, "that now I can—touch you?"

"It is . . . true," she answered.

"Tell me what you feel."

"I love you! I did not know that love could be so wonderful . . . so perfect . . . like music and . . . light."

"The light you have brought me, my *Drouska,*" the Prince said.

Then he was kissing her again—kissing her cheeks, her mouth, and the little pulse that was beating in her neck because she was so excited, and again her lips. . . .

A long time later he drew her to a sofa and they sat down together. His arms were still round her, as if he was afraid she might escape him.

"Hugo has told you what we have planned?" he asked.

"That we are . . . to be . . . married," Lokita replied, and her voice trembled with excitement, "but that it is to be a secret."

"Yes, a secret," the Prince said. "The only thing that matters is that you should be mine—mine—part of my heart and my soul as you were always meant to be."

"You said that when we . . . first talked together."

"And I meant it," the Prince said. "You made it difficult, very difficult to believe that I had not lost you, my darling, when you ran away before my party, but fate has brought us together again and that is all that matters."

"Was it . . . a very . . . lovely party?" Lokita asked wistfully.

"It was a hollow mockery without you."

"I . . . I am . . . sorry."

"You shall have a thousand parties," he said, "any party you wish, but for the moment I only want you alone."

"That is . . . what I want, too," Lokita murmured.

He pulled her closer to him, his hands caressing her, his lips moving against the softness of her skin.

Then he said with an effort:

"I must tell you what we have planned. We will be married in an hour's time, and I thought, Star of my life, my Dream come true, we would stay here tonight."

"If that is . . . what you wish," Lokita said. "You know I want to do what . . . pleases you."

"You please me," the Prince said fiercely. "Everything about you pleases, delights, and enthralls me. All I want to do for the rest of my life is to make you happy, to make you realise how much I need you, how completely we belong to each other."

Lokita gave a little murmur of happiness and hid her face against his neck.

He kissed her hair before he said:

"Hugo has offered us his house in the country, where we can go tomorrow and spend our honeymoon alone together."

Lokita raised her head and her eyes were shining.

"Perhaps we could ride?"

"We will do anything you want to do," the Prince answered, "as long as you let me make love to you and tell you how beautiful you are."

Lokita blushed.

"You know I . . . want that," she whispered, and she put her hand up to touch his cheek.

He took it in his and kissed the fingers and the palm as he had done before.

"I love you! I love you!" he said. "I shall have to teach you Russian, my darling, there are not enough words in English or in French to tell you of my love."

"I know a little Russian," Lokita replied, "enough to talk with Serge, but I am sure there is a great deal more you can teach me."

"There are many things I want to teach you, so many, my precious little flower, that it will take an eternity to come to the end of them. They all start with love and end with love."

He would have kissed her, but then he stopped himself.

"I was telling you what we will do," he said. "I have a feeling that in case Miss Anderson gets worse, you would not wish to go abroad for the moment."

"You are so . . . kind and considerate," Lokita whispered. "She is in fact very ill . . . and I am . . . afraid. . . ."

It was impossible to say more, for the Prince's arms were very comforting.

"I will look after you as she has looked after you," he said, "and one day perhaps all the secrets that you cannot tell me will be revealed to us."

"The secret of who I am?" Lokita asked.

"You are a very mysterious person," he replied with a smile.

"I think Andy is writing everything down," Lokita said. "Ever since we came to London she has been writing whenever she feels well enough, sheets and sheets of paper which she will not show me. They are locked away in a box."

"Then do not let us worry about them," the Prince admonished. "I want only to think about you, to ask you if you are happy and if you love me."

"You know I love you," Lokita said, "more than I can possibly put into words."

"Then tell me with your lips," he said, and his mouth came down on hers.

* * *

Lokita, followed by the Prince, moved from the Dining-Room into the Drawing-Room, which was a room she had not seen before.

It was filled with flowers and the scent of them made her feel that they were part of her love.

A servant brought a decanter of brandy and set it down on a small table.

"Is there anything else you require, Your Highness?" he asked.

"Nothing," the Prince replied.

The man bowed and went from the room.

Lokita turned from the vase of flowers she had been admiring.

"Come here!" the Prince said.

As if she was waiting for the invitation, she ran towards him, moving so lightly over the carpet that it seemed as if her feet hardly touched the ground.

He held her close against him but he did not kiss her, he merely looked down into her face to say:

"How can you be so beautiful, so perfect? I still cannot believe you are real, rather than a figment of my imagination."

Lokita gave a little laugh.

"I am real . . . and now I am . . . your wife. I never thought . . . I never dreamt when I first saw you . . . that I should wear your ring on my finger."

"You were hiding from me in the shadows as you have tried to do ever since, but now, my precious little white orchid, you can never escape me again."

"Do you think I would ever . . . want to?" she asked.

There was a little throb of passion in her voice that made him bend to kiss first her white shoulder, then run his lips over her skin to her neck.

He felt a little quiver of excitement run through her, then irresistibly his lips found hers and he kissed her passionately and demandingly.

Then, still holding her mouth captive, he picked her up in his arms and sat down in a big, comfortable armchair, cradling her against him as if she were a baby.

"This is how I have wanted to hold you ever since I first saw you," he said in his deep voice.

She laid her cheek against his shoulder and it was a gesture of endearment.

"The night we had supper with you after you had

rescued us from the bandits, I wanted you to . . . kiss me," she whispered.

"Do you suppose I did not wish it?" the Prince asked. "I have never in my life exercised such self-control."

"Why . . . did you not . . . do so?" Lokita enquired.

"Because I was afraid of frightening you, my *Drouska*. I knew you were mine, I knew that our hearts were beating in unison and our souls reached out towards each other. Yet I knew too that you were very young and very innocent."

She turned her face against his shoulder again.

"I want to be . . . sophisticated enough to know what you . . . want to make you happy," she whispered.

"You do that already by just being you," the Prince answered. "I wish I could explain to you in words, my darling, how different what we feel for each other is from what I have ever felt before. It is not a question of being sophisticated or unsophisticated, experienced or innocent. It is that you are the other half of me."

"Can that really be true?" Lokita asked. "You are so magnificent . . . so handsome and so . . . commanding."

"You are soft and sweet and very much a woman," the Prince said, and every word was a caress.

She felt his hands touching her and she quivered against him as if she were a musical instrument which responded to a player's sensitive fingers.

"I love you!" she said.

"How much do you love me?" he asked.

"All the world, the sea, the sky, more than Heaven itself," she answered.

"That is what I want you to say," he said. "I will teach you about love, my darling, I will make you love me until there is no world but me, no Heaven except in my arms."

There was passion in his voice and fire in his eyes. Then he was kissing her until the breath came quickly from between her lips and she felt little flames flickering through her whole body.

Suddenly she drew herself from his arms.

"I want to dance for you," she whispered, "as I used to dance for Papa, but this is more . . . wonderful and more . . . important because it is for . . . you."

The Prince drew in his breath.

"Dance, my precious!" he said.

She moved away from him into the centre of the room.

The light from the candles in the crystal sconces found shining lights in her fair hair, and her eyes were soft with love.

She stood still for a moment, almost as if she was listening for the notes of music which would tell her what to do.

Then she began to move slowly in the steps of a dance which the Prince had never seen before, but he knew it came from her heart and expressed the love he had aroused in her.

It was a dance of joy and of happiness that came not from the world but from the Divine.

Her arms went out to grasp the love that surrounded her, then almost as if it was inadequate without a blessing from above she reached up to the skies.

Then, just as she had done on the stage, she showed the Prince that she was not alone in her dancing but there was someone else with her, someone she loved, someone who had loved her.

She portrayed it so vividly, so compellingly, that the Prince found himself believing that Lokita was not moving alone but there were others beside and round her.

It was then, because their minds were so attuned to each other, that he knew she was thinking of his mother.

She conjured up the very spirit of her so that the Prince was vividly conscious of his mother's presence and it was almost as if he could hear her speaking to him.

The feeling was so strong and so unmistakable that

suddenly he rose from his chair and his voice rang out:

"Stop!"

As if he had brought her out of a trance, Lokita was suddenly still, her hands still outstretched towards what was invisible, her lips apart, her eyes looking into the unseen.

"I said stop," the Prince repeated in a strange voice, "because I cannot deceive you. I have to tell you the truth."

"The . . . truth," Lokita repeated, and it seemed as if her voice came from a very long distance.

"Yes—the truth," he said. "I love you, I adore you, I worship you! I am at your feet, but, my precious little flower, we are not married!"

She was very still but she did not answer and after a moment he said:

"I cannot marry you legally without permission of the Tsar, but I have dedicated my love to you. Every breath I draw belongs to you and I swear before God and on the memory of my mother that I will never fail you. That I will love and protect you until we both die."

There was a silence that was so intense that it seemed as if not only could they not speak but that neither of them could breathe.

Then almost as if he felt she was moving away from him, although she had not in fact taken one step, the Prince cried out, and there was a note of agony in his voice.

"If you love me enough, if you love me as I love you, it will not matter, it will make no difference. Love is greater than any laws that are made by man. Surely you must believe that?"

Lokita did not move but her hands dropped to her side.

She looked suddenly very small and very lost.

The Prince would have taken a step towards her but he checked himself and said:

"I have told you this because I love you, because I could not bear for there to be any secrets between us. Tell me that nothing matters except our love—tell me!"

The last words rang out commandingly. Then, in a whisper he could hardly hear Lokita said:

"I must . . . think . . . I must think . . ."

She put her hands up to her forehead, then turned and moved very slowly away from him across the room towards the door.

Chapter Six

Lokita walked slowly along the Boulevard de la Madeleine with Marie beside her.

She did not speak and Marie also was silent.

It seemed a century since they had left London to rush back to Paris and be in hiding once again as Lokita had been all her life.

Even now, after several days of trying to readjust herself to what was in reality her old life, she could not think of the Prince without tears coming into her eyes and her lips trembling.

"Why did I not do what he wanted me to do?" she had asked herself over and over again in the darkness of the night.

And the question hovered over her in the daytime so that it was hard to concentrate on anything except her own unhappiness.

When she had rushed blindly from Lord Marston's house, asking the footman in the hall to call her a hackney carriage, she had been a child seeking the help of the woman who had looked after her ever since she was a baby.

Only when the carriage actually reached the Boarding-House in Islington did she remember that she must not upset or disturb Andy, and thought frantically of what explanation she could make for returning home.

She had entered the house and, seeing no-one about, had run upstairs to Andy's room.

As she touched the handle of the door she drew in a deep breath and with an effort forced herself to enter quietly and calmly.

Andy was not asleep and she turned her head casually, obviously expecting to see Marie. Then when she saw Lokita she exclaimed:

"Why are you here? Why have you come back?"

Choosing with care every word she should say, Lokita moved towards the bed and knelt beside it.

"I came to ask your ... advice ... Andy dearest," she said in a soft voice.

"My advice?" Miss Anderson enquired.

"I do not know what to do or what would be right."

There was something so child-like and pathetic in the way she spoke that instinctively Miss Anderson put out her hand and laid it on hers.

"You are worried and frightened," she said as if she spoke to herself. "That is not what I intended."

"There is ... no-one I can ask but ... you," Lokita said.

"Ask about what?" Miss Anderson questioned, even though she knew the answer.

Lokita looked down at the white sheet.

"Lord Marston told me that you wished me to ... marry him," she said slowly, "but I cannot do ... that, Andy."

"Why not?"

"Because I do not love him, and he does not love me."

Miss Anderson did not speak and Lokita went on:

"I know how much Papa loved Mama. When he spoke of her his love vibrated from him, and you have always told me how much Mama loved him."

Lokita held Andy's hand in both of hers.

"How can I ... marry Lord Marston, or ... any man, unless I ... love him like that?"

"You have to be safe, my dearest," Miss Anderson replied, but her voice was uncertain.

"You would not wish me to be ... unhappy or ... afraid."

"Lord Marston is a gentleman. He would look after you."

"He does not love me as ... the Prince ... does."

The words were hardly above a whisper but Miss Anderson heard them.

"The Prince cannot offer you marriage," she said sharply.

"I can understand that," Lokita said, "but would it be ... wicked if I ... stayed with him as I ... want to ... do?"

"Neither your father nor your mother would ever forgive me," Miss Anderson replied, and now there was an inescapable pain in her voice.

Lokita raised her eyes and they were dark with suffering.

"Then what shall I do?" she asked. "You have always been so wise, you have always taken care of me. Tell me, Andy, for I cannot ... decide for myself."

For a moment Miss Anderson was still, then she said:

"Call Marie and Serge."

"But why?" Lokita asked, startled.

"Because I tell you to. I need them here this moment—immediately! We are returning to Paris!"

"To Paris?" Lokita could hardly breathe the words.

But from that moment, anything she said, her protests, her questions, her arguments, all were swept to one side.

Miss Anderson took the drops which Sir George Lester had given her and somehow Lokita and Marie got her dressed.

Little sips of brandy also helped, and Marie, being

French, believed it was more efficacious than anything any doctor could prescribe. It certainly sustained Miss Anderson during the long journey.

They left Victoria on a train that departed at seven o'clock and when they reached Paris Miss Anderson was in pain and seemed more dead than alive. Yet her will power sustained her and kept her going.

"Shall I tell the *cocher* to take us to our house?" Lokita asked as they installed Miss Anderson in a *fiacre* and Serge helped to pile the luggage on top of it.

"No!" was the reply. "We will go to *Madame* Albertini."

Lokita was surprised, but she was not prepared to argue with Miss Anderson, seeing how pale she looked.

Somehow she found the strength to explain to *Madame* why they had returned to Paris and to ask if she would take care of Lokita because there was no-one else to do so.

Madame was astonished to see them.

"How could you have gone away in that extraordinary manner?" she asked Lokita, her voice rising. "When you did not arrive at the Theatre on Monday, they all came rushing to me to ask what had occurred."

She threw her hands up in the air in a typical French gesture.

"What could I do, seeing that I knew nothing?"

"I am sorry, *Madame*," Miss Anderson said in a tired voice. "Lokita will explain why we went."

There was a pause before Lokita said in a low voice:

"It was because . . . Prince Ivan Volkonski was giving a . . . party for me and Andy did not . . . wish me to go."

"*La! La!*" she exclaimed. "I can understand that. The Prince has a reputation, and every night he had taken the Royal Box to watch you dance."

She gave a little laugh that was half a sigh.

"So that is why you ran away. I might have guessed it. *C'est toujours l'amour.*"

"It is always love!" Lokita repeated the words to herself then and every minute of every day that followed.

Love, love, love!

The words seemed to haunt her, just as when she lay crying at night she could feel the strength of the Prince's arms round her and the touch of his lips, which evoked sensations she had never known existed, not even in her dreams.

Her whole body ached for him. She felt as if her heart had been torn from her breast, leaving a gaping wound.

At the same time, she understood why he had told her the truth, and it was indivisibly linked with the reason why she had run away.

When she had danced for him she felt that her father was beside her, so close that he was as real as the Prince himself.

And with him had been someone else who she knew was her mother, even though it was difficult to visualise her face.

Then as she went on dancing there had been a third person, someone she knew did not belong to her but to the Prince.

And the love which came from this woman was as vivid and as real as the love of her father.

The Prince knew, he understood, Lokita told herself, and because their minds thought as one, neither of them could lie or fall short of the ideals of their parents.

It was love, true and perfect, which had drawn them together, and it was love, pure and sacred, which had driven them apart.

As she cried in the darkness of the small bed in the tiny room that she occupied at the top of *Madame* Albertini's house, Lokita prayed that one day she could see the Prince again, that one day it would be possible for her to belong to him physically as she did mentally and spiritually.

She and Marie turned off the Boulevard de la Madeleine to a side-street where *Madame*'s house was situated.

A tall grey house with wooden shutters, it was identical with all the others in the street.

Lokita opened the door because Marie was carrying a full shopping-basket and several parcels.

Inside, Marie turned towards the kitchen and Lokita ran up the stairs to a small room on the first floor, to where they had carried Miss Anderson the night they had arrived.

She heard voices before she opened the door and found, as she had expected, that *Madame* Albertini was talking away in her vivacious but sometimes shrill voice while Andy, lying back against her pillows, listened to her.

"Oh, there you are, Lokita!" *Madame* said as she came into the room. "I have just been telling Miss Anderson that despite the naughty way you behaved, *le Théâtre Impérial du Châtelet* is willing to have you in their next production."

"I cannot do anything until Andy is better," Lokita answered.

Her eyes met *Madame*'s as she spoke and knew she understood that it was not a question of when Andy would get better, but of when she would die.

It was impossible to leave her until that happened.

"That is what I thought you would say," *Madame* answered briskly. "But there is no hurry. You can take your time. I can assure you that *le Théâtre Impérial* is not the only one that wants you."

As if she was anxious to change the subject, Lokita held out the newspaper that she held in her hand.

"Here is *La Presse,* which you asked me to buy," she said to *Madame*.

"Good girl! I am glad you remembered," *Madame*

said. "I enjoy the gossip, which no other paper provides so well."

Taking the paper, she rose to her feet and added:

"*La Presse* informed me yesterday that your admirer, the Prince, has returned to his Château in the Champs Élysées."

Lokita was very still. Then she looked apprehensively at Andy, but the sick woman seemed not to have heard.

Her eyes were closed, and her cheeks were almost as pale as the pillows against which she was lying.

Quickly, having no desire to discuss the Prince, Lokita said:

"The news today is rather horrible. All the newsboys are calling out that the Grand Duke Frederick of Krasnick has been murdered by an anarchist."

Madame Albertini made a derisive sound.

"These anarchists!" she said. "They are a perfect menace! One never knows which Monarch will be . . ."

She was interrupted by a voice from the bed.

"Who . . . did you say had been . . . murdered, Lokita?"

"The Grand Duke Frederick of Krasnick. He was driving . . ."

"Let me see," Miss Anderson interrupted. "Give me the paper."

There was an urgent note in her voice and she held out her hand.

Surprised, *Madame* gave her the newspaper.

The murder was splashed over the front page:

GRAND DUKE SHOT BY ANARCHIST
Crowd tear assassin to pieces

Miss Anderson stared at the newspaper for what seemed a long time, then she said to Lokita:

"Fetch Prince Ivan here immediately!"

"P-Prince . . . Ivan?" Lokita repeated, finding it hard to say the words.

"You heard what I said. Go at once! Take Marie or Serge with you, but bring him back to me quickly. There is no time to be lost!"

As she finished speaking she seemed to collapse against the pillows, and Lokita said frantically:

"Her drops. *Madame!* Quickly! Her drops!"

Madame Albertini knew what to do and in a few seconds she was holding a spoon to Miss Anderson's white lips. As she did so, she said to Lokita:

"Do as you are told, *ma petite!* Fetch the Prince. I know she has something to tell him."

Lokita had not taken off her bonnet since she had returned with Marie and now she ran down the stairs. Finding Serge in the hall, she wasted no time looking for anyone else.

"Come with me, Serge!" she said.

He obeyed her as he always did without question and a few minutes later they were driving down the Boulevard de la Madeleine towards the Champs Élysées.

* * *

When Lokita had left the Prince, saying that she must think, he had sunk down in the arm-chair, fighting his inclination to pull her into his arms and plead with her.

He had intended never to reveal the truth, but everything that was sensitive and spiritual in his nature had responded to the inescapable feeling that Lokita had by her dance evoked the presence of his mother.

He had felt her near him as he had felt her at other times since her death.

Once when he had been in danger she had warned him. On another occasion, when he had been about to commit an act that was not worthy of himself or his rank, she had stopped him.

Her influence had always been far greater than anyone realised except the Prince himself.

The reason why he had never married, although
she had wished him to do so, was that he had never
found a woman with the deep, intrinsic goodness and
sensitivity of his own mother.

It was, he told himself now, the urgings of his soul
which had made him tell Lokita he was deceiving her
and prevented him from going on with the pretended
marriage.

"She loves me! I know she loves me!" he told himself as he waited for her return to the room where he
was sitting.

He thought he must let her think for herself and
realise the power of their overwhelming love for each
other.

Then she would know, as he did, that nothing else
was of importance and the only thing that really mattered was that they should be together.

On the mantelpiece the clock ticked the seconds by
and the Prince sat immobile, waiting and waiting.

It was over an hour later, when he could stand the
tension no longer, that he rose and walked into the
hall, preparatory to going upstairs to Lokita's bed-
room.

He could not believe that her door would be locked
against him and he was prepared now to go down on
his knees if necessary to beg her to stay with him because he could not live without her.

His foot was actually on the staircase when a footman on duty in the hall said:

"Excuse me, Your Highness, but will the lady be
returning?"

The Prince turned round, feeling as if the blood was
draining away from his body.

"What did you say?" he asked.

His tone of voice frightened the servant.

"Perhaps it was impertinent of me to ask Your
Highness, but the night-porter is old and deaf, and if

the lady was returning I thought I would wait up for her."

"You are speaking of Miss Lawrence—the lady with whom I dined and who is staying here?"

"Yes, Your Highness. She came out of the Drawing-Room soon after dinner and asked me to get her a hackney carriage."

"And you obtained one for her?"

"Yes, Your Highness."

With an effort the Prince controlled his voice.

"Where—did she tell it to—go?"

"I didn't hear, Your Highness. She spoke in a low voice to the coachman on the box while I was holding the door open."

The Prince felt as if he had turned to stone. Then when he reached the Drawing-Room, having no memory of walking there, he realised he had no idea where Lokita had gone.

There had been no reason for Lord Marston to tell him her address. He had merely said that Miss Anderson had sent for him.

When today he had gone, as the Prince had planned, to fetch Lokita to his house, he had not said where he was going.

The Prince put his hand up to his forehead as if he would force his brain to work clearly.

Lord Marston of course would know where Lokita was, and he was quite certain she had run like a child to the woman who had looked after her all her life and who was the only Guardian and protector she knew.

The Prince was also unaware of Lord Marston's whereabouts that evening.

When everything had been arranged as the Prince had planned for his and Lokita's false marriage, Lord Marston had said with a smile:

"As soon as this 'ceremony' is over, I will make myself scarce."

"Of course," the Prince agreed. "When shall I see you again?"

"Sometime tomorrow morning," Lord Marston replied casually. "There will be no need for you and Lokita to leave for Marston House until after luncheon. It will not take you more than two and a half hours to drive there."

If he had said any more the Prince had not heard it. He was concentrating with his whole being on Lokita and his love for her.

Now despairingly he found it impossible to think where or with whom Lord Marston might be staying.

If he had been in the same position he was quite sure there would have been a dozen women who would have welcomed him with open arms to their houses and to their beds. But as far as he was aware, his friend was not involved in any particular liaison.

There remained of course the possibility that Lord Marston had gone to one of his many Clubs.

These the Prince knew well, and ordering a carriage he drove from White's to the St. James's, and from the St. James's to the Cavalry, only to find that among the members in residence Lord Marston was not one.

By this time it was long after midnight, and, frantic though he was, the Prince dared not rouse the few of Lord Marston's relatives who he knew lived in London.

He could only go back to the house and wait with impatience and apprehension until the dawn came and he knew that only a few hours must pass before Lord Marston came home.

When Lord Marston returned at eleven o'clock in the morning he drove the Prince straight to the house in Islington.

"You are to stay in my chaise, Ivan," he said firmly as they drew up in the square. "If you rush into the house and upset Miss Anderson so that she dies, Lokita will never forgive you."

"I will wait here," the Prince agreed.

Lord Marston had looked at his friend anxiously.

He had known the Prince in many moods but the one he was in now was new, and it worried him.

Stepping out of his chaise, he walked to the Boarding-House, only to learn from the landlord that Lokita, Miss Anderson, and their two servants had left for Paris several hours earlier.

It was difficult to break the news to the Prince and even more difficult to keep him from shooting himself as he wished to do.

"I have lost her! I have lost her, Hugo!" he kept repeating over and over again. "I cannot live without her!"

It was his Russian temperament which made him take the blow more tragically and dramatically than any other man would have done.

Lord Marston gave him hope.

"If you are going to destroy yourself, Ivan," he said, "wait until after we have solved the mystery of Lokita. We know that Miss Anderson holds the secret of who she is, and we know too that she has committed her knowledge to paper."

He paused to say impassively:

"Whether she tells us or whether we read what she has written is immaterial. What is important is that we should be in possession of the facts."

"Suppose they are of no help?"

"I have a feeling they will be," Lord Marston said quietly. "No-one could meet Lokita without realising that she is a very unusual as well as a very beautiful person. When the truth is known, there may be a chance that you can marry her."

Lord Marston did not really believe this himself, but he had somehow to encourage the Prince and prevent him from putting a bullet through his head.

"We much go to Paris at once!" the Prince announced.

"I cannot leave until tomorrow," Lord Marston

objected, "because I have to see the Prime Minister this afternoon."

He wanted his friend to go without him, but the Prince waited and they set off the following day by the early train on which Lokita and Miss Anderson had left London the day before.

Their first call on the morning after their arrival in Paris was the house near the Bois.

The door was opened by the same old caretaker but he had no idea that the ladies had come back to Paris, and said that if they had, they had not got in touch with him.

"What shall we do now? What the hell shall we do?" the Prince asked as they drove away.

"We will go to the Theatre and see if they have any knowledge of her," Lord Marston said not very hopefully.

"Do that now!"

"At this hour?" Lord Marston queried. "You know as well as I do, Ivan, there will be no-one there, not even the cleaners."

The Prince bit his lip.

There were dark lines under his eyes which told Lord Marston he had not slept since Lokita had left him.

They drove round the Bois, the Prince looking amongst the trees and along the paths, hoping, Lord Marston knew, that by some miracle he would see Lokita riding towards him.

"I am getting hungry," Lord Marston said at length. "I am going to take you home, Ivan."

"I could not eat a thing!" the Prince answered.

"But I could!" Lord Marston said firmly. "And if you waste away from starvation you will be of no help to anyone, least of all to Lokita, should she happen to need you."

"She does need me! I know she needs me!" the Prince said fiercely. "It is only that damned Dragon who is keeping her from me."

Lord Marston remembered that when he had last seen Miss Anderson she had not looked at the least like the Dragon she was reputed to be.

Yet once again she had summoned up the power and the strength, which surprised him, to spirit Lokita away to some secret place where they could not find her.

They drove down the Champs Élysées and servants wearing the Prince's colourful livery opened the gold-tipped gates of the Château.

Outside the front door, Lord Marston drew the horses to a standstill, saying as he did so:

"I must say, Ivan, it is a great pleasure to drive your horse-flesh!"

The Prince was too sunk in gloom to reply.

He merely followed Lord Marston up the steps towards the front door. As they reached the top of them they heard a carriage coming into the drive behind them.

It was an open *fiacre,* and as the aged horse came to a stop behind the Prince's chaise, Lord Marston gave a sudden exclamation.

He had seen Lokita, but the Prince had seen her first.

In a second he had changed from a lethargic, unhappy man into one pulsating with excitement, and with his eyes alight he ran down the steps towards her.

"Lokita!"

Her name throbbed on his lips and as she looked at him her lips moved too, but no sound came from them.

The Prince put out his hands and her fingers were in his.

He crushed them painfully as if he had to reassure himself that she was real.

As he drew her from the *fiacre* she said:

"I have come to fetch . . . you. Andy has asked for . . . you. She wishes to see you . . . immediately!"

"To see me?" the Prince repeated.

The words were almost automatic, for his eyes were on Lokita's face and he was staring at her with such an expression of love and yearning that it made her tremble.

"Please . . . come," she said softly.

"Of course," the Prince answered.

His chaise was still waiting outside the front door, and, having heard what passed between them, Lord Marston got into the driving-seat and picked up the reins.

"Where are we to go?" he asked.

Lokita told him as if it was difficult to remember anything but that the Prince was beside her.

As they drove into the Champs Élysées, Lokita sitting between the two men, the Prince put his arm round her shoulders.

"How could you crucify me in such a way?" he asked.

"Forgive . . . me," she pleaded. "I went to Andy to . . . ask her advice and she . . . insisted on coming immediately to . . . Paris."

"I felt it must be something like that," the Prince said. "I could not believe that you had ceased to love me."

"You know I love you!" she answered. "It was agony . . . an agony I cannot describe . . . to leave you as I did."

They looked at each other, their faces drawn and lined with what they had suffered, and yet the love in their eyes illuminated them with a radiance which was blinding.

Lord Marston drove them swiftly and without speaking until they reached the street off the Boulevard de la Madeleine.

The groom travelling in the seat at the back of the chaise ran to the horses' heads.

Lokita led the Prince and Lord Marston into the tall grey house and up the stairs.

Only as they reached Miss Anderson's room did Lord Marston say:

"Perhaps she will not wish to see me."

"I want you to be there," the Prince replied. "I want you to hear what she has to say."

Lokita went into the room.

"I have found Prince Ivan, Andy," she said, "and Lord Marston is here too."

As she spoke, she saw that *Madame* Albertini was giving Miss Anderson some more of her drops in a spoon.

One look at her face told Lokita she was anxious.

"Come in!" Miss Anderson said, and now her voice was firm.

Madame Albertini moved away and Lokita ran and knelt down beside the bed.

"The Prince is here, Andy!" she said. "But if you are not strong enough to speak to His Highness he will wait."

"I have to speak—and now!" Miss Anderson replied.

As if they knew what she wanted, the two men each pulled a chair nearer to the bed, and *Madame* Albertini left the room.

The Prince was beside Lokita as she knelt on the floor, and Lord Marston's chair was on the opposite side of the bed.

"I have a lot to tell you," Miss Anderson began, "and very little time in which to say it."

Lokita gave a little cry.

"Andy!"

With what was obviously an effort, Miss Anderson laid her hand over Lokita's.

"Do not be unhappy, my dearest," she said. "I have done what had to be done, and I was afraid I would die before I could tell you the truth. Now I am released from my vow of silence."

Lokita looked up at her wide-eyed and Miss Anderson explained:

"It was a vow which I gave to your mother and father, and, thank God, I have been able to keep it."

Her voice was low but clear.

After a moment she went on speaking to the Prince.

"You have, I know, wondered who Lokita is and why there is so much secrecy about her. Well, now I can tell you. She is the daughter of Lord Leightonstone and Her Imperial Highness Princess Natasha!"

The Prince gave an exclamation.

"Can you possibly mean—my cousin?"

Miss Anderson nodded her head.

"Your cousin, Your Highness, daughter of the Grand Duke Boris."

The Prince stared at her incredulously.

"How can that be possible?" he began.

Miss Anderson put up her hand to silence him, then slowly and with difficulty she began to speak.

Sometimes her voice was so faint that the two men had to bend forward so as not to miss a word.

At other times it was as if some hidden strength within her gave her an inner power to speak clearly and almost forcefully.

It had all begun in 1847, when the Princess Natasha, one of the most beautiful girls at the Russian Court, had fallen in love with an unimportant young diplomat at the British Embassy called Michael Leighton.

They had met secretly and by some extraordinary good fortune no-one in the Winter Palace had any idea of what was happening.

Only Princess Natasha's Governess, Miss Anderson, who had looked after her since she was quite small, had been aware that her love for the young Englishman and his for her was becoming uncontrollable.

Tsar Nicholas ruled his relatives and his whole Court not only with a rod of iron but with a cruelty which made them all desperately afraid of him.

Because she was terrified that Princess Natasha would betray herself, Miss Anderson had agreed that they should leave St. Petersburg and go to Odessa, where the Grand Duke had built a Palace in the new Province of Bessarabia.

Even Miss Anderson had not known of the Princess's plan: when they were only fifty miles from the Capital, Michael Leighton should join them.

They were married in a small village by a Priest who had no idea of the Princess's importance and Royal blood.

They had travelled on together, and the journey, from being one of weariness and difficulties, had become weeks of unbelievable happiness and joy.

When they reached the peace and beauty of Odessa and were alone in the Grand Duke's Palace with only the faithful serfs to know what was happening, it was to the lovers a Paradise on earth.

Never had Miss Anderson known two people to be so happy or so wildly and overwhelmingly in love.

The excuse of ill health that had enabled Princess Natasha to seek the warm sunshine of the south also served Michael Leighton.

He excused himself from his diplomatic duties on the plea of illness, and it seemed to Miss Anderson that no-one remembered the two young people or cared what had become of them.

Natasha's father, the Grand Duke, had recently taken a new wife, who was jealous of her stepdaughter and was glad to be rid of her.

There was therefore no-one to ask questions or interfere, and when the following year Lokita was born, Miss Anderson became her only God-parent.

"You must look after Lokita as you have looked after me, Andy," the Princess Natasha had said in her soft voice, "and because she is born of love, perhaps one day she will be as happy as I am."

Because they were so desperately in love, the Princess and her husband left Lokita to Miss Anderson to look after, and were content to be alone with each other.

Then one day—one terrifying day which would always be engraved on Miss Anderson's mind—a servant whom they trusted arrived post-haste from St. Petersburg.

He had ridden by day and by night to reach them and was, he told them, only a little ahead of the *Cheka,* or Secret Police.

As she listened to what he had to say, Miss Anderson realised that all along they had been living in a Fool's Paradise.

It was inevitable that sooner or later the Tsar or those who toadied to him would become suspicious.

What they learnt now with growing horror was that someone had put the idea into the Tsar's head that his cousin Princess Natasha was not alone.

The Secret Police had orders to kill immediately any man who might be found with her, and there would be no question of his being able to ask for mercy or justice.

Frantic with fear not only for her husband but for her child, Princess Natasha insisted that he and Lokita should leave that very night in a ship that was sailing from Odessa to Constantinople.

Miss Anderson said she would go with them.

Carrying the baby in her arms, she left the Villa, unable because of her tears to see the face of the girl she loved and taught ever since she was a small child.

The agony of parting was almost too much for Michael Leighton, but he knew he had to save his daughter's life.

They left Constantinople as quickly as possible for Cannes, in the South of France, where Michael Leighton had arranged with Natasha to communicate with him.

He waited for a month before he received a letter. Then it came to him through the British Consul who had received it in the diplomatic bag from the British Embassy in St. Petersburg.

When he read what his wife had written to him, Michael Leighton nearly went mad.

The Tsar had made Natasha return to St. Petersburg because he had arranged for her marriage with the Grand Duke Frederick of Krasnick.

Natasha told Michael that she had pleaded with the Tsar, saying she could not marry a man she did not love, but he had merely ordered her to do as she was told.

As Michael Leighton knew only too well, if everyone did not obey the Tsar the moment he commanded it, he either sent them to Siberia or, worse, had them certified insane.

Natasha had no choice. To reveal that she was already married would have been to sign Michael and Lokita's death warrants.

It was Miss Anderson who finally convinced the distraught and despairing young man that the best thing he could do was to go back to work.

He had returned to London and had been appointed first to the British Embassy in Rome, then later to Brussels.

And it was Miss Anderson who decided it would be best for Lokita if they made their home in Paris.

She knew that it would be all too easy for people to learn details of a young diplomat's private life in Italy, in Belgium, and indeed in any Capital with the exception of Paris.

There, where every man, whatever his profession, was expected to have a liaison of some sort, no-one would think it in the least extraordinary if a house on the outskirts of the Bois belonged to a young Englishman.

Michael Leighton rose rapidly in the diplomatic world. He was knighted before he died and became Lord Leightonstone.

Only Miss Anderson knew how cruelly he had suffered at the thought of the woman he loved with all his heart being married to another man.

Just once was Natasha able to see Lokita, and that was after she had been the Grand Duchess of Krasnick for over five years. She let Michael Leighton know that she was going alone to Odessa for a holiday.

What it must have meant for her to see her real husband again, and for Michael to hold her in his arms, was impossible to describe.

As Miss Anderson's voice faltered and there was a sudden mist of tears in her eyes, those listening to her knew how emotional that meeting had been after the yacht had anchored in Odessa Harbour late one night.

The Grand Duchess of Krasnick had died when Lokita was fourteen, but still there was need for secrecy.

Tsar Nicholas had in 1855 been succeeded by his more liberal-minded son, Alexander II.

There was no longer the fear of the Secret Police finding out about Lokita and murdering both her and her father, as would have happened in the past, but the Grand Duke was still alive and there could be a scandal which would affect the Monarchy of his and Natasha's country.

Miss Anderson had therefore been tied to her vow, but she had known that her life was ebbing to a close and she must protect Lokita's future.

Desperately she tried to marry her to Lord Marston, feeling that if she was married to an Englishman as her mother had been at least she would be safe from the type of dissolute men who would pursue her only for her beauty.

What she had not anticipated was that Lokita, like her mother, would fall wildly and overwhelmingly in love the moment she saw the man who was meant for her by fate.

Frantically Miss Anderson had tried to fight both the Prince and Lokita! But now as she came to the end of her story, her voice very weak and hardly audible, there was a smile on her lips.

"Now that you know the truth," she said to the Prince, "can you put things right for Lokita in the future?"

The Prince bent forward to take Miss Anderson's hand in his.

"I can only thank you," he said in his deep voice, "for all the love and all the care you have given Lokita. I know that when he hears what has happened, the Tsar will grant us permission to marry. I will devote my life to her, and I will leave for Russia tonight."

He bent his head and kissed Miss Anderson's hand and he felt that for a moment her fingers tightened on his.

Then she turned her face towards Lokita's and even as she did so there came a little gasp from between her lips and her body seemed to sag against the pillows.

For a moment even Lord Marston did not understand what had happened, then Lokita gave a cry that seemed to ring out in the room.

"Andy! Andy!"

It was the cry of a child who is lost in the dark. Then the Prince's arms were round her, holding her, comforting her.

Chapter Seven

"I remember it . . . I do remember it!" Lokita exclaimed.

She was standing on the deck of the yacht as it moved into Odessa Bay, and Lord Marston, standing beside her, smiled at her excitement.

The Harbour was certainly very beautiful in the sunshine and beyond it they could see the Colleges, the Opera House, and the fine new buildings that had been built by Prince Voronzov when he had become Governor-General of New Russia and Bessarabia.

He had been sent to the south to create a new Province by the Tsar and it was only then that his brilliant powers of organisation were realised.

No architect could have had a finer terrain for his plans, and with the repopulation of the desolate Steppe country north of the Black Sea and the introduction of steam navigation, the land round Odessa flourished.

As they came towards the beautiful city, Lokita remembered that Lord Marston had told her how the Prince had imported English cattle and caused numbers of French vine-culturists to stock and supervise the new Crimean vineyards.

She had been deeply interested in everything Lord Marston said because it was impossible for her thoughts to wander even for a few minutes from anything which concerned the Prince.

All the time they had travelled from Paris to Odessa it had seemed to Lord Marston that her love and her beauty increased together day by day, until he wondered if it was possible for there to be a lovelier woman in the whole of the world.

The Prince had kept his promise to Miss Anderson and had left for Russia almost immediately after her death.

It was Lord Marston who had supervised the funeral and had comforted not only Lokita but also Marie and Serge.

It was when they had come back from the little English cemetery that he told Lokita what the Prince's plans were for her.

"As soon as you feel like travelling," he said, "we are journeying to Marseilles, where his yacht will be waiting for us."

"Where are we going?" Lokita asked, and her eyes, which had been dull with weeping, had a new light in them.

"Somewhere you have been twice before in your life, although I doubt if you will remember much about it," Lord Marston replied with a smile.

"Odessa!"

Lokita had hardly been able to breathe the word.

Lord Marston nodded.

"The Prince has a Palace there but he has not spent much time in it in the last few years."

"Odessa!" Lokita said almost beneath her breath, and Lord Marston knew she connected it not only with her father, whom she had loved so deeply, but also with her mother.

They had however stayed in Paris for a short while so that Lokita could buy clothes.

On her behalf Lord Marston got in touch with her father's Solicitor and found there was quite a large sum of money waiting to be claimed and an allowance that would be paid to her every month.

It was very small compared to what the Prince had already settled on her when he had arranged their pretended marriage.

Lord Marston, however, did not refer to this, but merely told Lokita that she could spend any sum she wished and he would arrange the payments.

She had gone to Worth's because no-one else in Paris had such imagination or could create the fairy-like quality in his gowns which Lokita portrayed in her dancing.

From the first moment she met the famous English Couturier, he had concentrated all his brilliance on creating a frame for her unusual beauty.

Worth had just decreed that the crinoline, which had lasted for eight years, was to disappear, and now the gowns were swept to the back, and the materials, fragile lace, tulle, and satin, were particularly becoming to Lokita.

Because she was choosing gowns she would wear for the man she loved, she was not only patient during the long fittings but when it was finished gave every gown she wore a mystique that no other woman could have achieved.

Looking at her now with her fair hair glinting in the brilliant sunshine, the pale green gown she wore echoing the green of her eyes, Lord Marston thought that if the Prince was an exceptional personality Lokita was no less outstanding.

He had loved the Prince ever since they had been boys together, and he knew that in Lokita his friend had found someone not only worthy of him but who would develop the deep potential in his character which was still dormant.

"Can we go ashore?" Lokita asked eagerly.

"We must wait for our instructions," Lord Marston replied with a smile.

At every port at which they had stopped on their

way to Odessa, there had been letters from the Prince with flowers and gifts for Lokita.

She was so eager to hear from him that whatever time of day or night they arrived, however early in the morning, she was always on deck waiting for the messenger who she knew would be standing on the Quay.

The letters came to them by express train, but to Lokita they were as exciting and romantic as if they had been conveyed by horses galloping over wild, uninhabited country.

She almost expected to see the messenger gallop into the Quayside standing up in the stirrups, the reins held in his teeth, and flourishing a *Kindjal* or *shashka* in each hand.

It was the way, Lokita knew, the Caucasian guards known as the "Furious Eagles" showed off their wonderful feats of horsemanship, and Lord Marston had described to her how he had seen the Prince ride with his troops in just such a manner.

The letters, when she received them, however they were conveyed, brought a flush to her cheeks and a happiness to her eyes that gave her a new beauty.

Never had she thought to receive such eloquent love-letters, written with such force and power that it made her feel as if the Prince was beside her speaking the words in his deep voice which made her heart vibrate to his.

Not only his letters but the flowers which waited for her in an almost overwhelming profusion held a special message that only she could understand.

Star-shaped orchids, pure lilies, roses in bud, tuberoses, jasmine, and white lilacs, they all meant something to her personally and the Prince spoke to her through them.

There were presents, too, such as she had never dreamt she might possess—rows of pearls, small and perfect, which seemed to glow translucent against her skin.

Three little diamond brooches fashioned like butterflies, in a case, with nothing flamboyant about them such as the one he had offered her before they had met, but exquisite in every detail—masterpieces in miniature.

At one port of call there was a small bird-cage, and the bird, which sang when a small lever was pressed, had been made by a master-hand of precious jewels.

Now the yacht was tied up against the Quay, the gangplank let down, and resplendent in the Prince's livery a messenger came on board.

Before he could present what he held in his hand, Lokita asked impulsively:

"You have a letter from His Highness?"

"It is here, Knyīeza," he answered, addressing her in the same way that Serge had always done.

He gave a large envelope into Lokita's hand, then bowing presented another to Lord Marston.

Lokita ran into the Saloon so that she could be alone.

Her heart was beating and her fingers were trembling as she opened the envelope.

She had expected a long letter but there were only a few words.

Tonight, my darling, my love, my Star whom I worship, we shall be one.

Ivan

She kissed the letter and pressed it against her breast.

She was standing, her face radiant with happiness, as Lord Marston came into the Saloon.

"He is here!" Lokita said before he could speak. "Can we go ashore and see him now?"

"I have been given very detailed instructions as to what we are to do," Lord Marston replied, "and I think the Prince is obeying the old superstition that a bridegroom should not see his bride on their wedding-day before they meet at the altar."

"We are to be . . . married . . . today!"

Lokita could hardly breathe the words.

"This evening," Lord Marston answered, "and judging by the boxes that are being carried aboard, the Prince has sent you a number of presents."

"I only want . . . him," Lokita said almost beneath her breath, but Lord Marston heard.

"From what he wrote to me, he is as impatient as you are."

"Oh, Hugo!" Lokita exclaimed. "Do you think my gown is beautiful enough? Suppose when he sees me again he is disappointed?"

"I do not think you need worry about that," Lord Marston replied, remembering that the Prince's words had seemed almost to burn the paper.

Despite the fact that it seemed to Lokita a very long time before eventually they could go ashore, there was a lot to do.

The Prince's presents, she found, included jewellery that left her breathless.

There was for her to wear at her wedding a Russian tiara designed in the traditional style that was like a halo encircling her head from one ear to the other.

It was fashioned of stars set with diamonds, and to wear round her neck there was a necklace in the same design.

As if he had anticipated that the jewels she would wear would be magnificent, Mr. Worth's design for Lokita's wedding-gown had been comparatively simple.

Of the finest lace, it revealed the soft curves of her figure, so that from the front she looked like a Grecian goddess and at the back there was a long train frothing out in soft frills surmounted by a large bow of white satin.

It made Lokita look very young and very ethereal, but when her jewels were added she looked resplendent and, as Lord Marston told her—Royal.

"That is in fact what you are," he said.

She looked at him enquiringly and he explained:

"The Tsar has not only given his permission for you to marry the Prince, but by a special *Ukaze* to the Senate you have been given the name and rank of Princess Lokita Kurievski. It is of course a name in your mother's family."

Lokita clasped her hands together.

It was difficult to explain even to Lord Marston how much this meant to her.

Because her existence had been secret for so long, she had felt that the Prince was in fact marrying beneath him, someone of no account, someone to whom his family would condescend.

But now she was acknowledged in her own right and she knew that she could hold her head high and not be ashamed of her background.

It had been exciting and in some ways a relief to know that in fact, as her father's daughter, she was the Honourable Lokita Leighton, a name which until now she had never been able to use. But she was now also a Princess, the equal of the man she was to marry.

And although she told herself that where the Prince was concerned it was not of any consequence, it would affect her status in Russia and, she told herself with a little blush, it would make things easier for their children when they had them.

Finally Lokita, fussed over by Marie, was ready and she went into the Saloon where Lord Marston was waiting and sipping a glass of champagne as he did so.

He too was looking unusually handsome and resplendent, and Lokita's eyes widened at the sight of him.

She had never before seen him in his diplomatic uniform.

With his silk stockings, his knee-breeches, and his gold-embroidered coat, he looked as her father had when sometimes he had left the little house in the Bois to go to the British Embassy or to the Tuileries.

Then she had been left behind, but now this evening

she was to step into a new world, a world into which never before had she even crossed the threshold.

"You look very lovely, Lokita!" Lord Marston said.

"Do I really?" she asked.

He knew she was not fishing for compliments, but anxious that she would be in every way perfection for the man who would be waiting for her.

"I cannot believe that anywhere in the world there could be a more beautiful bride!"

The veil Lokita wore did not cover her face but hung from her tiara over her hair at the back and reached to the floor.

It seemed to almost envelop her like a cloud, and Lord Marston was sure that the Prince would feel she was in fact a goddess come down from the sky to be his bride.

He gave a glass of champagne into Lokita's hand.

"Drink a little," he advised, "because although it will not be a long Service, it will be, I am sure, something of an ordeal."

"All I am thinking of is that I shall see ... Ivan," Lokita murmured.

"I am sure he is thinking the same thing," Lord Marston declared.

As if she suddenly remembered, Lokita said:

"In case I overlook it later, Hugo, I want to thank you now for all your kindness to me. No-one could have been more understanding or more marvellous than you have been."

Lord Marston smiled.

"I have been wondering as we travelled here together whether it was a compliment or an insult that Ivan trusted me alone with you."

Lokita gave a little laugh.

"He knew you were his friend and that I could never look at any man except him."

She paused and her eyes were very soft as she went on:

"But although my heart belongs to Ivan, there is a special place in it which is always yours."

The way she spoke was moving and Lord Marston lifted her hand to his lips.

"I am only hoping," he said, "although I feel it is optimistic to do so, that one day I will find a wife who is not only as lovely but also as sweet as you."

"Oh, Hugo, I hope so!" Lokita said.

They smiled at each other, then Lord Marston picked up the wrap that went with Lokita's gown and put it over her shoulders.

The heat of the day had passed but it was still very warm and the sun glinted on the roofs and spires of Odessa, turning them to burnished gold.

Lord Marston walked with Lokita down the gangplank and there waiting for them was a *troika* not only elaborately carved, painted, and gilded, but also decorated with flowers.

It was drawn by four magnificent horses with flowers in their manes and garlands round their necks.

"How pretty!" Lokita exclaimed breathlessly.

As Lord Marston helped her into it, the crowd which had gathered on the Quayside cheered and wished her good luck.

"I can understand everything they are saying to me," Lokita said excitedly.

She had been studying Russian during all the voyage and had talked with Serge for several hours every day.

It was obvious, Lord Marston thought, that she had an aptitude for languages, which was not surprising.

At the same time, Russian was complicated and difficult, especially with the various dialects, and he himself had always been grateful for the fact that the Russian aristocracy invariably spoke French.

But Russian was to Lokita part of the Prince and she was determined to be exceedingly proficient in everything concerned with him.

The *troika* drove off at a speed that was characteristic, and now they could see flowers everywhere and dominating everything were the tall, lofty, romantic cypress trees.

The first two had been planted by the Empress Catherine on the journey with Potemkin to her southern possessions. From these trees were grafted all the many cypress groves and alleys which had come to be typical of the Crimean landscape.

They passed through the city and now they were out in what Lord Marston had always thought of as a fabled land, radiant and improbable.

They drove along the coast. Then suddenly, rising one hundred and fifty feet sheer above the Black Sea, Lokita saw the Palace, its roofs and towers gleaming above the trees encircling it.

At the sight of it she drew in her breath and Lord Marston could understand that she was moved by the beauty of it, as indeed he was.

Silhouetted against the gleaming gold and crimson of the setting sun, it had a splendour and at the same time a beauty that made it seem to have been transported straight from a tale of the *Arabian Nights*.

Now the *troika,* moving at an almost incredible speed, swept in through some great gates and up a broad drive which was bordered with brilliant flowers and shrubs in every colour.

Then there were pillars and marble steps and the Palace seemed overpoweringly magnificent, and yet it had a charm that was somehow intimate and inescapable.

There were rows of liveried servants and a Major Domo resplendent with gold braid to escort them.

The marble, lapis lazuli, onyx, jasper, and malacite of the interior of the Palace and its treasures were almost obscured by masses of white flowers.

It was all enormously impressive and Lord Marston felt Lokita's hand trembling a little on his arm as they followed the Major Domo through halls and down wide corridors.

Then there was the sound of music through the open doors of a Chapel and the aroma of incense.

A servant came forward to hand Lokita a bouquet and she took it from him, dropping her eyes as if she was suddenly shy and a little afraid of what lay ahead.

Lord Marston covered her hand on his arm with his in a gesture of reassurance, then very slowly they moved forward into the Chapel.

The music seemed to swell into a paean of thanksgiving. There were the seven gleaming silver sanctuary lamps, a blinding array of candles, flowers, the Priests' embroidered vestments, and ikons.

Lokita raised her eyes to the Prince.

He was waiting for them at the altar steps and Lord Marston, who had seen the Prince in many different uniforms, had never seen him look so magnificent.

He wore the long becoming tunic, clasped high at the neck, which was traditionally Russian, but it was white, and white fox-fur encircled the hem of it where it reached his hips.

His breast blazed with decorations and gave him an authority and an air of importance that was awe-inspiring. Yet Lokita, looking at him, was conscious only that he was there and she loved him.

She saw the fire in his eyes and knew that he had hungered and longed for her in the days they had been apart, which at times had seemed interminable.

The Service began, then Lokita knew as they said their marriage-vows that they were encompassed about with those they loved and who loved them.

She felt that her father and mother were beside her and that Ivan's mother was with him, and as the Priest joined them in marriage they were there and the whole Chapel was filled with love and the glory of God.

They clasped the lighted candles, the two crowns were held over their heads, and finally they were blessed by God and the Church.

Then when the Prince drew Lokita down the short aisle and back into the Palace, everyone seemed to disappear and they were alone.

He did not speak, he merely took her into a room that was circular in shape and decorated with the star orchids which meant so much to both of them.

The delicate flowers covered the table, climbed up the walls, and hung in wreaths from the ceiling.

The Prince drew out a chair so that she could sit down at the table, then he sat down beside her and his eyes looked into hers.

"My—wife!"

He said the words beneath his breath, and yet she heard them.

There was the music of violins, but they could not see the musicians. The servants who brought them food wore white.

Lokita had no idea what she ate and drank, she only knew that her whole being was throbbing because the Prince was beside her, and even if they spoke commonplaces to each other every word had an inner meaning so that her heart spoke to his heart, her soul to his soul.

Afterwards she remembered nothing he said in actual words.

Yet she felt that she told him her whole life-story until they had met and how she had missed him and longed for him during what had seemed to her to be a voyage centuries long from Marseilles to Odessa.

At last the meal was finished and the servants withdrew and they were alone. The Prince sat back in his carved arm-chair surmounted with a cross, and lifted a glass to his lips.

"I have dreamt of seeing you here," he said softly, "as my wife and my love, knowing that we have a whole life-time in front of us."

"What did the Tsar . . . say?" Lokita questioned.

She supposed it was a question she should have

asked before, but somehow it had seemed unimportant.

"His Majesty was very understanding," the Prince answered, "and now there is always a position for you at Court, not only as my wife but as your mother's daughter."

"There will be no . . . scandal?"

The Prince shook his head.

"You need not be afraid of that. An explanation has been found for your presence. I do not wish to bother you with it for the moment. I want only to talk about—us."

His voice deepened on the last word and now Lokita's eyes fell before his because she was shy.

"We have so many important things to say to each other," the Prince said. "Shall we go where we can talk without being distracted? Where I have made, my beautiful darling, a special place for you and for our love?"

Lokita looked at him enquiringly and he rose from the table, holding out his hand, and she put hers in it.

There was a long French window in the room opening onto the garden.

The Prince drew aside the lace curtains which covered it and Lokita stepped out onto the terrace to find that the sun had sunk below the horizon and there was only a faint glow of crimson left.

It was dusk and the stars were just coming out in the sable of the sky overhead and the garden was full of mystical shadows and music.

It was the music Lokita recognised as belonging to gypsies, with none of the wild high notes of their violins but the tinkle of cymbals and the melody of the accordians.

Then as she stood there beside the Prince, her hands resting for a moment on the stone balustrade, suddenly as if at some given signal the garden came to life.

Lights began to glow in the distance, to flow nearer

and nearer in a strange way which she had been told by Lord Marston was something that had been achieved in the gardens inside the Winter Palace.

But this was outside, and it was impossible to think that anything could be more beautiful as she realised gradually that the whole garden in front of her was planted with arum lilies and they were lit from beneath.

Now she could see that the flowering shrubs which encircled the rest of the garden were all white—everything was white and pure and had, Lokita knew, a special meaning for them both.

"It is ... lovely! So very ... very ... lovely!" she said.

"Like you, my precious flower," the Prince answered, "and tonight, as there is no Russian party like the one you missed in Paris, I have created a background for your beauty and perfection."

She looked up at him with a little smile and he said almost fiercely:

"You are perfect—perfect as no other woman has ever been. As I have told you before, there are no words in which I can tell you what you mean to me."

Lokita felt herself tremble because of the passion beneath his words and now he drew her along the terrace and down the wide steps into the garden.

They moved to music which made her feel as if she danced on air through the fragrant lilies and she thought they were like an enchanted sea and that she and the Prince too were enchanted.

They walked among the illuminated blooms and through the shrubs to where at the far end of the garden, out of sight of the house, there was a small white Pavilion.

It was not made of marble as she might have expected, but of a special precious stone that had been quarried in the Urals and was so rare, so beautiful, that it reminded her immediately of the petals of a star orchid.

The Prince drew her inside and she saw that in the centre of the Pavilion was a large room with only three walls and where the fourth should have been there was only the night.

Below it was a sheer drop to the sea and the vista in front was of the horizon merging with the sky and it was impossible to know where one began and the other ended.

For the moment Lokita was spellbound by what she saw in front of her. Then she realised that the room, like the one where they had dined, was decorated with white flowers, but these were not orchids but roses and tuberoses, the flowers of passion.

The only piece of furniture in the room was a huge couch covered with white petals. From the ceiling above their head, every few seconds more petals, soft and scented, floated like a message of love to the ground.

The scent of the flowers combined with the music which throbbed in Lokita's head made her feel more excited than she had ever before felt in her life.

The light, which was hidden and dim, came from behind the walls, but it was just strong enough for Lokita to see the Prince's face and the expression in his eyes.

As she turned to look at him, the words she was about to say died on her lips, and she could only feel that without even moving she reached out towards him and became a part of him.

"I love you!" the Prince said hoarsely. "How am I to tell you how much I love you—how much you mean to me?"

"I am so . . . afraid that I am . . . dreaming," Lokita whispered. "Only a dream could be so beautiful, and . . . you could be . . . there."

"I am here!" the Prince said.

Slowly and as if he forced himself to be very gentle, he put out his arms and drew her to him.

He looked down into her eyes but he did not kiss her

as she had expected. Instead he took the diamond tiara and the veil from her head and threw them carelessly to the ground amongst the petals.

He undid her necklace, then raised his hands to pull the pins from her fair hair so that it fell over her shoulders. As it did so she felt him draw in his breath.

"That is how I have wanted to see you," he said. "This is how I want you, and I have never been so afraid in my whole life as I was when I thought I had lost you."

"We have not . . . lost each other," Lokita murmured. "We are . . . married and I am your . . . wife."

She said it almost wonderingly, conscious of the ring that encircled her finger, and finding it hard to believe that she really had a name, an identity.

She belonged to someone she loved and he need not be ashamed of her.

As if he knew what she was thinking, the Prince said:

"The past is over. Forget it. There is so much, heart of my heart, my perfect love, in the future for us both."

He touched her hair.

"I have so much to make up to you for," he said, "for the years of loneliness, the uncertainty, the fear, the secrecy which every woman hates, but most of all, my precious darling, because you were afraid of what the future might hold."

"But I . . . found you," Lokita said softly, "and now you are my . . . future. All that happened in the past I can forget."

"I will make you forget it," the Prince replied. "I will make you remember only that I love you and that we belong to each other. That you are mine now and for all eternity."

He pushed back her hair from her shoulders and bent his head. He did not kiss her skin as she expected but moved his lips over the softness of it.

It had excited her before when he had touched her

fingers with his mouth, but now it sent thrill after thrill coursing through her.

Somehow it was intermingled with the music and the fragrance of the flowers to make her feel she was no longer herself and had no identity apart from him.

As the Prince felt her tremble not with fear but with the intensity of her feelings, he exclaimed triumphantly:

"I excite you, my beloved little flower!"

Lokita blushed.

"I love . . . you," she whispered.

There was a note in her voice which brought the fire flaming to his eyes and broke the spell that had bound them since the vows they had exchanged in the Chapel.

The Prince's arms tightened and now his kisses became masterful and insistent.

He kissed her shoulders, first one, then the other, then her neck, intensifying the thrills and the excitement she felt, and lastly her mouth.

She felt as if he was like a tempest rising slowly and growing stronger every second, until finally when his lips held hers captive she was swept away by a whirlwind.

It was so powerful, an irresistible force, and yet it was a rapture beyond words, almost beyond thought.

She knew that the Prince's iron control which had prevented him from touching her until now had been broken.

She felt too as if all the inhibitions and the anxieties and even the shyness which had held her like little fetters were broken.

This was life, this was a love so omnipotent, so overwhelming, that she could only acknowledge its majesty.

The Prince's kisses became more passionate, fierce, and demanding, and yet she was not afraid.

She surrendered herself utterly to him, giving him

not only her body but her heart, her soul, and her mind.

She no longer existed as an individual, she was his, subservient to his will and glorying in his supremacy.

"I love you! God in Heaven, how I love you!" the Prince exclaimed.

Now Lokita felt him undoing her gown and as it slipped to the ground like a shaft of moonlight he lifted her in his arms.

He carried her to the petal-strewn couch and laid her down gently to stand for a moment looking down at her. At her fair hair streaming down over her nakedness, at her eyes wide and soft with love, at her lips trembling for his lips.

"I love you!" the Prince said again, but she was not certain whether he spoke in Russian, French, or English.

The language they used was the language of the gods, and the love they expressed with their lips, their hearts, and their bodies was the manifestation of love which both men and gods have used since the beginning of time.

"You are mine!" the Prince exclaimed. "Mine from the top of your shining head to the soles of your tiny feet. I worship you, my lovely darling! At the same time, I want you as a man wants the woman who is his!"

"I want you . . . too," Lokita wished to say, but the words were lost against his mouth.

She felt his hands touching her and something wild and wonderful within her body rose like a flame to echo the fire she could feel on his lips and in every breath he drew.

She knew this was part of their love, as sacred and perfect as the feelings she had felt when she raised her arms to the stars.

It was love, all-consuming, all-demanding. A love that swept away not only barriers but all reservations, all restrictions.

The Prince's lips were fiercely demanding, and she

knew there was nothing of her that did not belong to him, just as the wild and wonderful passion she evoked in him was part of her.

"I love you, my precious, my *Drouska,* my flower, my wife!"

She could feel his heart beating against hers and she thought there was another light that gleamed in the room besides the light behind the walls.

It was the light of love, the light that was Divine, the light that came from their souls. . . .

"I love . . . you . . . I . . . love . . . you."

"You are mine! Give me yourself."

"I am . . . yours . . . yours."

"My flower—my little Star—my Soul!"

Then there was only the murmur of the sea, the petals falling softly from the ceiling and the stars coming out one by one in the great arc of the sky to be reflected in the water beneath them.

ABOUT THE AUTHOR

BARBARA CARTLAND, the world's most famous romantic novelist, who is also an historian, playwright, lecturer, political speaker and television personality, has now written over 200 books. She has also had many historical works published and has written four autobiographies as well as the biographies of her mother and that of her brother Ronald Cartland, who was the first Member of Parliament to be killed in the last war. This book has a preface by Sir Winston Churchill. Barbara Cartland has sold 80 million books over the world, more than half of these in the U.S.A. She broke the world record in 1975 by writing twenty books, and her own record in 1976 with twenty-one. In private life, Barbara Cartland, who is a Dame of the Order of St. John of Jerusalem, has fought for better conditions and salaries for Midwives and Nurses. As President of the Royal College of Midwives (Hertfordshire Branch), she has been invested with the first Badge of Office ever given in Great Britain, which was subscribed to by the Midwives themselves. She has also championed-the-cause for old people and founded the first Romany Gypsy Camp in the world. Barbara Cartland is deeply interested in Vitamin Therapy and is President of the British National Association for Health.